Groundwood Books is grateful for the opportunity to share stories and make books on the Traditional Territory of many Nations, including the Anishinabeg, the Wendat and the Haudenosaunee. It is also the Treaty Lands of the Mississaugas of the Credit. In partnership with Indigenous writers, illustrators, editors and translators, we commit to publishing stories that reflect the experiences of Indigenous Peoples. For more about our work and values, visit us at groundwoodbooks.com.

THE BUTTERFLY'S STING

THE BUTTERFLY'S STING

ABBIE HARLOW

Groundwood Books
House of Anansi Press
Toronto / Berkeley

Published in 2025 by Groundwood Books / House of Anansi Press
groundwoodbooks.com

We gratefully acknowledge for their financial support of our publishing program the Canada Council for the Arts, the Ontario Arts Council and the Government of Canada.

Canada Council for the Arts | Conseil des Arts du Canada | ONTARIO ARTS COUNCIL CONSEIL DES ARTS DE L'ONTARIO an Ontario government agency un organisme du gouvernement de l'Ontario | With the participation of the Government of Canada Avec la participation du gouvernement du Canada | Canada

Library and Archives Canada Cataloguing in Publication

Title: The butterfly's sting / Abbie Harlow.
Names: Harlow, Abbie, author.
Identifiers: Canadiana (print) 20250136562 | Canadiana (ebook) 20250136589 | ISBN 9781779460011 (softcover) | ISBN 9781779460028 (EPUB)
Subjects: LCGFT: Novels.
Classification: LCC PS3608.A745 B88 2025 | DDC j813/.6—dc23

Design by Greg Tabor
Cover photograph by Ground Picture / Shutterstock
Printed and bound in Canada

Groundwood Books is a Global Certified Accessible™ (GCA by Benetech) publisher. An ebook version of this book that meets stringent accessibility standards is available to students and readers with print disabilities.

Groundwood Books is committed to protecting our natural environment. This book is made of material from well-managed FSC®-certified forests, recycled materials, and other controlled sources.

FSC www.fsc.org MIX Paper | Supporting responsible forestry FSC® C016245

For Grammie

Love you more!

ONE

"Fists up."

I raise my gloved hands. Elbows low and tight to my torso, guarding my stomach and ribs. Fists by my head, chin ducked. Left foot and arm forward, the hard surface of the ring beneath my feet, steady and sure. When I breathe in, there's the scent of dust and old paint and sweat, leather and canvas and more sweat.

"Three minutes," Jack says from somewhere to my left, on the edge of the ring. The sun isn't up yet, and the only lights in the gym are the ones right above the ring, above me. "Focus on your footwork. Keep your stance narrow and stay light on your feet. And remember that right arm. Don't drop it when you slip."

I nod. My feet bounce, itching to move again.

Stretches. A mile run around the neighborhood. Some light jump roping, a few hits on the heavy bag. Finishing with this: shadowboxing. All of it's a much gentler workout than usual. Enough to loosen my muscles and get my head right, but nothing that will tire me out too much — or worse, injure me — before tonight. Now is only a trailer to the main event.

But my little brother, Zach, had another nightmare last night. And Kate, my younger sister, slept through it all, like always, so I stayed up alone, trying to calm him down. Failing. Letting him crawl into bed with me, even though he's grown at least an inch since we moved in here and the two of us don't really fit in a twin bed anymore. And once Zach finally dozed off again, then *I* couldn't sleep. Tossing and turning. Running through the checklist in my head over and over, doing the math for the millionth time, every calculation adding another pound to the invisible weight on my chest till I felt pinned to the bed. Breathing as slowly as possible to keep the panic down, down, down.

After a night like that, no amount of time in the gym ever feels like enough.

Beep. Jack's phone timer. "Go."

I've barely started when the timer sounds again.

"Bo," he snaps. Most of his face is in shadow except for his mouth, twisted in its usual scowl.

It takes everything in me not to reply "Jack" in the same snotty tone. But the bruise on my chin hasn't completely faded yet. Tonight will give me enough to deal with without adding something new from Jack, too.

"What did I say," he adds, "about dropping that arm?"

"I didn't —"

"'I didn't,'" he mimics. "Is that a joke? Your hand was by your hip. Do you even *want* to compete tonight? Should I call Tyler and tell him you're dropping out?"

Breathe in through my nose. Out through my mouth.

Four months. That's all. Get through the tournament, and it's over.

"Sorry," I say finally.

"Show me you mean it. Do it again. Really watch that arm this time."

Beep.

The moment Jack says "Go" again, I turn my attention to my shadow on the ring floor and picture my opponent. What he might be like. Small for a guy, but still bigger than me, because they're always bigger than me. Fast. With a cross I don't want to take unless I feel like immediately losing and spending the weekend with a killer headache and even more bruises than usual.

Jab, slip, hook. Hook, uppercut. Feint, hook. Endless combinations of hits and tricks and dodges, back and forth and around the ring in an endless dance. Turning my hips for a better angle, a faster turn, or a stronger punch, pivoting, ducking my head to avoid a blow — all while doing my best to keep my stance narrow and feet light, like Jack said. Air bursts from my mouth with each imaginary hit, the puff of breath and the shuffle of my shoes on the canvas the only sounds in the whole world.

Beep.

I lean forward, hands on my knees, looking around the gym while I catch my breath. It's still too dark to see much, but after a year of daily training here, it's all so familiar. Punching bags of every shape lining the walls: classic long heavy bags, smaller tear-shaped speed bags, accurately named wrecking-ball bags, a blocky uppercut bag bolted to the back wall. A low, long shelf of free weights in every size. Jump ropes. Heavy-duty foam mats if you need to spar and the ring's taken. Spare gloves and hand wraps and headgear, disinfected nightly by Jack himself, or by me when he's in a foul mood.

Off the main gym there's a smaller room with dumbbells and a few crappy weight machines, a tiny locker room, and Jack's office, the door closed and locked. Cheap blinds cover the big windows that face the street. I don't need the sunrise or the lights on to see the faded and chipped paint, the rusted door hinges, the scuffs and dents on the floorboards.

The sound of shoes shuffling on the ring floor. Jack, moving from his usual spot in the corner to join me.

I straighten, eyeing my uncle the way I would an opponent. Six-foot-two frame, almost half a foot taller than me. Biceps straining against shirtsleeves. Eyes the color of stone — Mom's eyes, without any of the crying or the laughter. Arms crossed, fingers curled.

And that scowl.

I swallow. I didn't drop my arm so much in the last round, did I? Jack didn't say anything about it when the timer stopped.

But when it comes to my uncle, that doesn't necessarily mean anything.

Silent, Jack stops right next to me. Too close to only be giving the usual end-of-training notes. He raises his hand.

Instinctively, I wince. My shoulders tense. I turn my head, bracing for the pain —

Jack's hand on my shoulder — once, twice. The kind of congratulatory gesture he makes when one of his typical — aka adult, buff, male — students does well.

But I still flinch.

Jack doesn't seem to notice. He's smiling at me. His teeth flash like a vampire's.

"You're ready."

***

Like always, I help Jack prep the gym for its 6:00 a.m. opening. Turn on the lights. Put equipment away. Gather my gloves and headgear and water bottle. Wipe down the ring floor, removing any sweat or spilled water. Erase any evidence that I was here at all this morning, basically.

It's not illegal for Jack to teach me boxing. But the reason why he's teaching me definitely is, and I'm not Jack's usual clientele. Better to keep a low profile.

When that's done, Jack goes to his office, and I unlock the plain, almost-invisible door at the back of the main gym. That door opens into a narrow hallway lined with bikes and another door. Behind *that* door is a narrow staircase that leads to the apartment above the gym. Jack's apartment.

Our apartment, I guess. But calling it that still feels weird.

As I reach the little landing by the front door, I hear the faint *ding!* of the bell above the gym's entrance, announcing the day's first customer.

Good. That will keep Jack downstairs for a while.

I put my gear away. Take a cold shower to keep the muscle soreness at bay. Get dressed. Carefully apply makeup to the small yellowed bruise on my chin till it's erased and it's safe for me to wake up Kate. I listen to Kate sing in the shower while I coax a sleepy Zach out of bed. Then it's time for breakfast.

Sometimes I wonder where Jack gets his ideas about what families do. With Mom and Dad, "family breakfast" meant eating Pop-Tarts and bananas in the car on our way to school. And I doubt Mom and Jack — Mom's younger brother — ate breakfast together with their parents, because Mom always got sad when she talked about Grandma and Grandpa. We never met them. Even though we all lived in La Salida, Kate, Zach, and I had never even met Jack until he showed up at Dad's funeral two years ago, his arm in a sling and his face bruised (a sparring lesson gone wrong, I found out later).

Not exactly the kind of family you picture eating a nice breakfast together like people do in movies.

But for whatever reason, Jack wants Kate and Zach and me to have breakfast together. A full-on meal at the table, the four of us, every day. Even on weekends. Or busy mornings before school.

"PB&J or turkey?" I ask Zach as he and I head to the kitchen.

He doesn't answer right away — not until he's looked all around the living room and joint dining room/kitchen. His eyes pause on Jack's empty seat at the table and the closed front door, before moving to Kate. She's at the stove, food and dishes already laid out all around her. I don't know how she always manages to get completely ready for school *and* start cooking in the same time it takes me to talk Zach into brushing his teeth, but she does.

Zach exhales quietly.

"What are you gonna have?" he finally replies, dropping his backpack on the floor by the kitchen table with a soft *thud*.

The label on his T-shirt is sticking out. I tuck it in, smooth the collar. "Turkey."

"I want turkey, too. But no tomato. Tomatoes are gross."

I salute him. "Aye, aye, captain."

My nine-year-old brother smiles, showing the gap in his top row of teeth. Zach looks like me, like Mom. Wavy dark hair and a thin face and a slightly too-long nose. He's a little pale, and there are bags under his eyes. Otherwise, there's no trace of the kid who fell asleep curled up at my side last night, sniffling and shaking.

I join Kate at the counter. My sister is two years younger and two inches shorter than me, blonde, with big eyes and a dimple in her left cheek — a duplicate of Dad so good, she could have gone through a copier. She's wearing sky-blue jeans and a white shirt, and her cheeks are inexplicably streaked with blue and white face paint, her hair pulled up in a giant blue scrunchie.

She flashes one of her sunny smiles at me. Looking at a smile like that, you'd think we *did* have one of those movie-perfect families.

After a year and a half with Jack, the three of us work like a well-oiled machine. I prep lunches. Zach sets the table. Kate cooks. Today it's scrambled eggs, sautéed zucchini and peppers, and wheat toast — the healthy kind that tastes like cardboard. Protein and vegetables and good carbs — food that will give me energy for tonight's fight without making me slow or sleepy.

The air smells like coffee and peppers and olive oil. Kate hums beside me. I brush Zach's hair with my fingers.

For the first time since Zach woke me up last night, I feel still.

"Here, Zach, go put these on the table," Kate says, handing him a stack of plates from the cabinet — he's not quite tall enough to reach on his own yet.

As soon as Zach's busy with the dishes, Kate jerks her head in the direction of the front door.

"Scale from one to ten?" she whispers, like she does every morning after training. Jack's moods aren't what anyone would call predictable, but how he acts in training is usually a good indicator of the rest of the day.

"Three," I whisper back. "Maybe two?"

"Awesome." Kate's face lights up. "Hey. Are you gonna see Pretty Boy today?"

My cheeks warm. I carefully layer tomatoes on my sandwich. "I told you not to call him that. It's weird."

"It's accurate. You know he's obsessed with you, right?"

Before I can tell her she's delusional, I hear the sudden pound of footsteps on the stairs. The key in the lock.

Immediately, Kate goes back to cooking. I return to sandwich construction. Zach runs back into the kitchen and darts between me and Kate, close enough that I hear him breathing.

Whack.

I jump a little, but it's only Jack slapping the morning newspaper on the kitchen table. *La Salida Times*. It might be the last newspaper on earth to actually print on paper, and Jack might be the last person on earth who actually reads it.

"Good morning!" he says, downright chipper.

"Morning," Kate replies, visibly relaxing.

"Morning," Zach squeaks, so quietly that only I hear it.

Jack gets an empty mug and busies himself with the coffee maker.

"Did Bo tell you about her stellar training session this morning?"

"No." Kate glances at me. *Definitely two*, she mouths.

"No! Well." Jack claps me on the shoulder again before taking a sip from the mug. "Couple of minor bumps, but it was only a warm-up. She's ready for tonight. More than ready. I pity the sucker they pit against her."

"He's exaggerating," I tell Kate.

"I never exaggerate." He turns his attention to me. "I want

you home right after school. You're sleeping until dinner, and we're going over early. Got to scope out the —"

His cell starts ringing. Jack sets his mug on the table and picks up the phone. "Jack Nielsen speaking."

"He's … energetic today," Kate whispers, cracking an egg.

"That's one word for it," I mutter.

"Must be a family trait." She laughs. "Remember how Mom would get?"

Yeah. But where Jack's energetic because he's riding a post-training high that won't last, Mom could go like that for days — till she crashed and spent the next week in bed, or till Dad convinced her to start taking her medication again, and she evened out.

Till Dad died. Then there wasn't anybody who could convince her, so Mom never took it.

But I don't want to mention any of this while Zach's in earshot.

"I'm just glad someone called him," I say instead. "If I have to hear that speech one more time …"

"What's to scope out, anyway?" Kate asks. "It's the same every time, isn't it? Bunch of buff dudes and you?"

I glance down at Zach, still hovering near me. We try not to talk about the fights in front of him.

"Who was that one guy?" she continues, oblivious. "Bicep Billy?"

She laughs. Something in me grates, like a knife skidding across a plate wrong.

"It's not funny," I say. "Tonight's important."

Kate tips the eggs into the pan. "I was teasing. Relax."

How can I relax? I mean, okay, she's got a point about the other fighters. They *are* a bunch of angry buff dudes, and most of their ring names are stupid. But tonight's not just any fight. It's the *tournament*. If I win tonight, I go to the next round. And if I win again, then I go to the next round. And if I do that three more times, then I *win*. Win the whole tournament, get the grand finale cash prize, $25,000, split sixty-forty between Jack and me. Way more money than the $200 I get for winning a regular fight.

And if I win ...

We'll finally have enough to leave.

Kate and Zach and me.

But none of that happens if I don't win tonight.

So, no. *Not* the same.

"Hey." Kate bumps my hip with hers. "I know. Really. Okay?"

I take a breath, then bump her hip back. "What's with the face paint?"

She gives me a funny look. "It's for the pep rally."

"What pep rally?"

"Basketball. You know. The big rivalry game against Franklin? They've announced it, like, every morning this week," she adds when I stare at her blankly. "The game's right after school. Don't worry, I'll be back in time to make dinner."

Something in me stings. I thought tonight, of all nights, Kate would want to come home right after school. Be with Zach and me. I try to tell myself it's good that Kate's busy, that she has plans. When we were in foster care, she was so angry, she'd snap at anyone who so much as looked at her. All her friends scattered. I didn't know if she'd ever find new ones.

As I turn to the kitchen table, I brush against the newspaper Jack brought in. It flutters to the ground.

I pick up the paper — only to have an all-too-familiar face staring up at me. A man with wavy dark hair and vaguely unfocused eyes. Beneath the mug shot is a caption: *Derek Lee, 31, arrested last night on charges of DUI and drug possession.*

My heart stutters.

"Zach," I say carefully. "Why don't you get your shoes on?"

Zach doesn't ask questions. He disappears to the back of the apartment before Kate hisses, "What's wrong?"

I shake my head, gesturing for her to keep cooking. Jack's still on the phone.

My eye snags on a small, faded picture in a clean white frame hanging on the wall right next to me, showing two kids. A boy and a girl, arms around each other. Jack must be around Zach's age, Mom a couple of years older. Jack's hair is long, wavy, and falling over his forehead instead of shaved close to his scalp. He's smiling. And Mom — teeth flashing, cheeks dimpled. She doesn't look like someone who'd grow up to abandon her three kids, but people are full of surprises, I guess.

I have this urge to go back downstairs, to hit something.

When Jack finally gets off the phone, I practically push the newspaper in his face. "Did you see this?"

"Of course I saw it. Tyler called me." Jack snatches the paper from me and folds it up again.

"Well, you didn't tell *me*."

Jack slaps the paper down on the table next to his coffee mug. "Medic — or Derek, whatever you want to call him — is an idiot, and it finally caught up to him. What do you care?"

"Well," I say, working very hard not to sound snarky, "for one thing, I can't fight tonight if my cutman is in *jail*."

"Tyler's talking to his contacts. You'll have a replacement by tonight."

"What about the police? He got arrested. And what about the —" I stop myself from saying *fight club*. Jack hates when I call it that. *We aren't a bunch of anarchist psychos*, he likes to say. "The ring? What if they —"

"Are you kidding? Did you actually read what it said?" Jack taps the paper. "He got caught driving high. That's nothing to do with us. Besides, Tyler's got so many contacts in the police department that even if they did find something, it'll get squashed."

My hands flex at my sides. "I just think —"

"I advocated for you with Tyler," Jack snaps. "I stuck my neck out to get you in this tournament because *you* insisted. And the $250 buy-in I paid for you isn't refundable. So if you're trying to back out now —"

"I'm not! I just don't want to get *arrested*."

"What did I just say?" His voice rises dangerously. "No one's getting arrested."

"But —"

BANG.

CRASH.

Kate yelps. I stare at Jack's fist, still on the table where he slammed it. Knuckles white. Mug in pieces on the floor, the biggest shard by my left foot. Coffee splattered over the rug like a crime scene. Long brown splotches stain my white shoes, my jeans.

Not a two.

Kate's frozen, spatula hovering over the frying pan. I hope she doesn't overcook the eggs. That'll only make things worse.

"Look what you made me do," Jack snaps, standing up. His white T-shirt is splattered with coffee, but he's looking at the broken mug. "And on a fight night. What would we have done if you'd cut your hand?"

My hands are shaking.

Jack pinches the bridge of his nose, like I'm giving him a headache. With a sigh, he reaches out and wraps an arm around me, pulling me close. I swear I can feel Kate holding her breath behind me. Feel air hitching in my lungs.

"We're family, Bo," Jack says. "True family sticks together. Protects each other. No matter what. You know that better than anyone. Right?"

I try not to look at the picture of Jack and Mom on the wall behind him. "Right."

"So you don't need to worry about this. Don't get so worked up. Now go get your brother. It's time for breakfast." Jack half pushes me away. "I'll clean this up."

Zach is sitting on the very edge of my bed, shoes on, his library book clutched to his chest. He looks seven again, like we just got the news about Dad.

Zach hiccups, the way he does when he's nervous. "What happened?"

"Oh, nothing." I dig through my dresser for fresh clothes. "Mug fell and broke. Got coffee all over me."

I pick a new pair of jeans, a new T-shirt and change in the bathroom. When I return to the room, Zach's exactly where I left him.

"I heard Jack yelling," he says.

I drop my clothes in the laundry basket. "You know how he gets. It was just a mug falling. Really."

When Zach still doesn't look convinced, I sit on the bed next to him. He scoots close to me. The look on his face is so sad and serious that I feel that weight on my chest again.

It's getting harder to shield Zach from it, to explain things away the way I've tried ever since we moved in with Jack.

Gently, I brush Zach's hair out of his face. Mistake. There's a thin scar by his hairline. It's mostly white now, but the sight still sends me back. A year and a half ago. The three of us in separate foster homes, waiting for Jack's emergency guardianship paperwork to be approved. The night Zach ran away to try to find me. The night he got hit by a car. The phone call. The hospital. Kate crying. Me, crouching in the hospital bathroom alone, head between my knees, hands numb, feeling my chest move while also somehow feeling like *I'm not breathing I'm not breathing I'm not breathing* —

One of the greatest boxers of all time, Muhammad Ali, had this specific fighting style. He'd bounce a lot, move a lot, stay just out of reach — and then he'd go in fast, striking sharp and quick and hard, sometimes taking his opponent out in only a few hits. When he was asked to describe this style, he said simply, "Float like a butterfly, sting like a bee."

I close my eyes. *Float*. My heart thunders against my chest like it's trying to burst out of a cage. I think of the sound my knuckles make when they hit the bag, of the apartment search page open in an incognito window on my laptop, of the Book hidden safely in the zippered compartment of my backpack.

I think of the Plan. *Our* plan.

To get away from Jack for good.

TWO

Like always, we bike to school.

Me in the front, Kate in the back, Zach in the middle. We ride away from Jack's apartment in the middle of the island to the beach, biking past gray sand and single-story ranch houses and low-hanging cypress trees. The road's clogged with cars: parents driving carpools, commuters trying to get to the bridge or the ferry to go off-island for work. In the weak sunlight, the San Francisco Bay gleams blue and green and gray, a mood ring that can't settle on a color. Across the bay, San Francisco itself appears fuzzy and distant, still shrouded in morning fog. Sharp, cold wind stings my face, smelling like water and sand and salt.

I won't miss much when we leave. But I will miss this wind, this view, this smell.

We stop in front of Zach's school, La Salida Elementary. Zach pulls at his bike lock and stands up.

"Can we go to the library today?"

It feels like there's a lump in my throat. It took us a whole three months to notice the pattern. Jack does something. To me. And immediately, Zach wants to go to the library, his favorite place. With me. Only with me.

"Don't you have, like, a hundred books checked out already?" I say.

"Not a *hundred*." He laughs. "Please?"

"I have a match tonight." I glance around, even though I remind myself that it doesn't matter if anyone's listening. Officially, the story is that I participate in amateur boxing tournaments out of town. ("The best lies are always a little bit true," Jack says.) It's what we tell Zach, too. But it still feels like something I shouldn't talk about in public. Like if I say it too much, someone will see right through the lie. "Remember?"

"Oh." Zach's face falls. "Right."

"Monday after school. I promise. Okay?"

He doesn't smile, but he grabs my hand and squeezes. "Okay."

After Zach goes inside, Kate and I ride another half mile along the perimeter of the island until we run into a series of single-story white stucco buildings lined with big windows: La Salida High, the island's only high school. A long line of cars leads to the drop-off zone and the parking lot. Some students hang around outside, but most rush into the warmth of the buildings. Kate and I are the only ones at the bike racks.

"Don't worry about Zach." I'm gripping my backpack straps so tight, my fingers hurt. "I'm getting us out. Soon."

Kate kneels to lock up her bike. "Yeeeeeah. Okay."

I frown. I don't know why Kate says it like that, like she doesn't believe me. Zach may be in the dark about this — we didn't want to risk him accidentally telling someone, didn't want to get his hopes up too early.

But Kate *knows* the Plan.

It was her idea. Our first few weeks with Jack were actually okay. Good, even. He bought us all new bikes. Took Zach to his follow-up doctor's appointments and helped him get back to sleep after a nightmare. Made dinner, bringing in me and Kate to help, teaching us recipe after recipe, joking around the entire time. I mean, he's Jack, so he was intense and a little weird about everything. But he didn't yell. Didn't lose his temper.

There was even a night when I was helping Jack with dinner and I got this awful wave of homesickness, of missing Dad and even Mom. I didn't say anything. But Jack put his arm around me and said, "I know exactly how you feel." I almost burst into tears over the lettuce I was chopping.

Then, about two months in, I burned the chicken for dinner. Jack had been in a bad mood for a couple of days. Kate and Zach were in their rooms. It was only Jack and me in the kitchen.

I didn't even see him move.

Jack apologized right away. Said he was just hungry after a long day at work, and now I'd burned the chicken, so of course he'd gotten frustrated, but he hadn't meant to snap like that, and wouldn't I forgive him, keep this between us?

I told myself it was a one-time thing. An accident. He'd apologized immediately. It didn't leave a bruise. And he was my uncle. If I told anyone, he'd get in trouble, and then what would happen to us?

But it happened again. This time it *did* leave a mark. The social worker was coming the next day — her monthly check-in, making sure we were okay — so I watched a makeup tutorial on YouTube so I could hide the bruise.

When she asked how I was doing, I smiled and said, "Great."

The third time, Kate saw.

After that, I knew we couldn't stay. But we didn't have any other family to go to. The police couldn't find Mom. Dad was dead. Our grandparents were dead, too. There were no long-lost aunts or distant cousins. There was only Jack, which was how we'd ended up with him in the first place.

Kate and I stayed up half the night Googling our options.

Report Jack to our social worker or the police? No way. We'd get put back in foster care. Most likely separated again. I thought of the scar on Zach's forehead, still red and angry then. I wouldn't do that to him again. To any of us.

Try to run away? Too easy to get caught and sent back to Jack, who wouldn't be very forgiving. Or, worse, labeled as "not thriving" with Jack and sent back to foster care.

Get emancipated? Kate and Zach were too young. I'd have to leave them. Even if that was an option, I'd need Jack's signature to get emancipated, which he'd never agree to.

That left Kate's last, desperate idea. She'd tugged on my arm at 2:00 a.m. and whispered it. *Leave on your eighteenth birthday*. I'd be a legal adult, old enough to become her and Zach's legal guardian and get all three of us out of here.

No more Jack. No more adults keeping us apart.

"You could take care of us," she whispered. "We don't need anyone else."

It was like standing in a dark room and having someone turn on the light. *Of course*.

That was a little over a year ago. In that time, Kate and I (well, me, mostly; Kate's usually busy with cheer and work) have done a ton of research, a ton of planning. The details may have changed since that night — we won't be leaving *on* my eighteenth birthday, for example — but the basic idea is the same.

Now, I let myself picture it. The truck I'll buy with my savings. Kate in the front seat and Zach in the back and everything we own wedged in the truck bed. The radio up loud — louder than Jack would ever allow — and Jack himself nowhere in sight. Alone at home or, better, locked up. The three of us smiling. The *bump, bump, bump* of the grooves in the metal bridge beneath the tires as we drive to the mainland.

It's not that it won't be tricky. Of course it will. But we know the system, and we've planned for everything.

The Plan can't fail.

Well. Unless I lose tonight.

I kneel next to my sister. "I mean it, June, we're out of here. We just have to get through the rest of the school year."

Frowning, Kate opens her mouth, but is interrupted by Sabrina Carpenter suddenly blasting behind us. When I turn around, I see a beat-up minivan pulling up in the drop-off lane. The girl in the passenger seat is swaying to the music, and the movement in the back seat tells me she's not the only one.

"Oh! That's Emmy's car." Kate jumps to her feet, brushing dirt off her jeans. "I gotta go."

"Kate —"

But she's already gone, rushing to join the group emerging from the back of the minivan. They're all in blue and white with face paint that matches Kate's. They throw their arms around my sister, pulling her toward the school's main doors. She goes with them without looking back.

***

The pep rally that's apparently been announced all week is held at the end of the school day. When the bell rings, teachers usher everyone toward the gym, making sure no one ditches. In the gym itself, hand-painted banners in sky blue and bright white hang above the doorways. Smiling student council reps direct us to the bleachers and ask us to squeeze in so there's room for everyone. The floor gleams. The room echoes with laughter and shouting and Olivia Rodrigo crackling through the PA and that really specific shoe-squeaking sound you only hear in school gyms.

It's a complete waste of time. But it's a mandatory waste of time, so I deal. Ignoring senior class StuCo rep Sam Soya directing me to the third row, I take the bleachers two at a time till I get to the very top, where I park myself in the far corner.

I pull my laptop from my backpack and open the incognito window to my spreadsheet: The Plan.

There are ten tabs: Timeline, Savings, Guardianship, Lawyers, Cities, Schools, Housing, Jobs, Utilities, and To Buy. Everything we need for the Plan. Each tab is color-coded, full of links and notes and calculations.

It's risky, keeping this in writing. But becoming a legal guardian at eighteen is complicated enough, let alone planning a multi-person escape from your crap uncle. It was too hard trying to remember all the details, and I didn't want to miss something important. So, spreadsheet it is. I only ever open it in incognito mode, when Jack isn't around, and the whole document is protected with a password only Kate and I know.

On the Housing tab, I enter the info about the apartment complex I researched before bed last night. The Crossing. It's about an hour and a half away from here, in a town way less expensive than La Salida. The building is old and small, and the pictures make it look a little run down, but it's not like we need a penthouse. And it's cheap. It's at least worth a second look in March or April, when it's time to start making decisions.

Suddenly, the music pauses, and our vice principal's voice crackles all around. "Welcome, Sharks, welcome to the pep rally! We'll be starting in just a few minutes! Please, everyone file in as quickly as possible."

The benches in front of me fill up. I put my laptop away. I spot Kate down in the first row of the same bleacher section as me, already in her cheer outfit. She's laughing hysterically at something, surrounded by a knot of other cheerleaders looking at her like she's the center of the universe.

My row is still empty. But I turn my phone screen brightness down anyway as I search *Derek Lee arrest La Salida.*

The *Times* article pops up first:

JANUARY 25: Police arrested a La Salida man (31) on possession of drugs, possession of drugs with intent to distribute, possession of an unregistered firearm, driving under the influence, reckless driving, and resisting arrest. A witness called 911 after the man allegedly ran a red light on Pebble Street and clipped a passing car, nearly pushing it into opposing traffic. When police arrived on the scene, they found a "rather large quantity" of drugs as well as a firearm. The suspect fled but was caught and arrested after a brief pursuit on foot. The man has been identified as Derek Lee, a longtime La Salida resident with one prior arrest for shoplifting in 2019.

"It's miraculous that Mr. Lee did not severely injure himself or anyone else," said La Salida Police Chief Liz Flores. "We intend to investigate this matter fully, and we hope that our partners in the DA's office will prosecute to the fullest extent of the law."

I lean against the wall. Maybe Jack was right. I mean, "we intend to investigate this matter fully" doesn't sit great with me. But it's not like she said they were going to investigate his entire life, only this incident. And it's true that Tyler has friends at the police station — I've seen them at the warehouse, betting mostly — who'd do anything he asked to keep the ring a secret. I'm sure they're the reason we haven't been shut down already. And Derek's been going to the warehouse for years without getting caught.

As long as no one gets too curious —

"Hey, Bo!"

Crap. I lock my phone and shove it back in my pocket.

"Liam! Hi."

Liam Covey looks the same as ever. Pink cheeks, suntanned skin. Honey-brown eyes and honey-brown hair sticking up slightly at the back. Double-knotted black Converse, Carhartt pants, and navy-blue sweatshirt with MILLS COLLEGE printed on the front in butter yellow. A smile that's big and effortless and weirdly … familiar. Not familiar because I know him. Familiar in some other way that I can never place and always bugs me. Like when you recognize a melody but can't remember the name of the song.

Liam points to the empty space next to me. "Can I sit here?"

I swallow the question I want to ask: *Why?* Liam has plenty of friends, and none of them are friends with me. We've never hung out outside of school. All I know about him, really, is that he loves peanut M&M's, and his mom's a police dispatcher.

Not exactly my vibe. Especially now.

But ever since we were mock trial partners in government last semester, Liam's been around more. Saying hi in the hallway. Inviting me to sit with him and his friends at lunch or go to the beach with them after school. I always find a way out of it — *I have to study for this test, I have training, sorry* — but none of my go-to excuses will work at a pep rally.

Reluctantly, I nod. Liam sits. Behind him, students file in, encouraged by Sam Soya, who asks everyone to squish together because space is tight.

By the time the rally actually starts, Liam's arm is flush against mine and the corner of my phone is digging into my thigh. He smells like soap and some spice I can't name.

Suddenly I can't remember if I put deodorant on today or not. I did. Right?

"Hey," Liam says. "You've got something on your chin, I think?"

"Thanks." I duck my head, pretending to wipe my chin. *Stupid*. I knew I should have checked my makeup after lunch.

I prop my elbow on my knee and rest my chin in my hand. Gesture to his hoodie. "So you ... uh ... want to go to Mills?"

"Yeah, I wanna be a doctor, and they've got this premed program that's really —"

Liam's phone lights up.

He glances at the name on the screen. Swipes right so fast, he nearly drops the phone.

"Dad! Hi! Hi. How are you?"

The PA crackles. "*PLEASE WELCOME THE SHARKS SPIRIT SQUAD!*"

Echoing applause, whoops, shouts. Liam raises his voice. "Dad? Dad? I can't hear you! I'm at a spirit rally, I'll call you after!"

Liam pockets his phone. I swear he's sitting up straighter. He's definitely smiling way more when he turns to me and says, "Listen, I was gonna text you. A bunch of us are going to the game, and then we're getting burritos at Sal's after. You should come with."

"Oh. I don't —"

"C'mon. You can't say no to Sal's. And everyone would love to see you."

That seems like a stretch. La Salida High is just big enough that ninety-five percent of Liam's friends probably don't even know who I am. The five percent who do — Izzy, Carmen, Aaron — were in my old friend group. But none of them have really talked to me since Dad died in a car accident nearly two years ago. It was awful for all of us, but I guess it was most awful for Mom. She barely left her bed, let alone the house. Barely spoke, except to snap at one of us for making too much noise. Or to sob.

"Mom's not feeling well," I told Kate and Zach every day as I made grilled cheese for dinner for the fifth night in a row, figured out her Wells Fargo password and muddled my way through paying bills online while the bank account quickly drained, replied to texts on her phone, pretending to be her. "She'll be better soon."

But weeks went by, and Mom only got worse. Snapped at us all day. Cried all night. By July, she was gone. Kate, Zach, and I woke up one morning and found her closet cleaned out, the driveway empty, Mom nowhere, and a note on the table: *I can't do this without him. I'm sorry. I love you.* I remember feeling the words like a sucker punch but also feeling a strange kind of relief. Like some part of me had always known that this was how it would end.

While the police looked for Mom, Kate, Zach, and I went into foster care, scattered across the East Bay. Zach stayed in La Salida. Kate went to Berkeley. I was in the Oakland Hills. We could visit each other, but we weren't together. It was supposed to be temporary until Mom came back, or the cops found her and *brought* her back. But when Mom stayed gone — the cops had footage of her crossing from California to Nevada, but they lost track of her after that — we were told the new plan was for us to live with our uncle, who'd agreed to take all three of us, though we'd need to wait for a judge to approve his emergency guardianship application before we could move in with him. I'd just turned sixteen.

We spent five weeks in foster care. That doesn't sound like a lot of time until you're spending every minute of it wanting to cry or scream, or feeling nothing at all. Or hating your mom so much you could punch a wall, then missing your mom, then hating her again. And always, *always* worrying about your siblings — your sister's silence and anger, your brother's tears, counting down the seconds until you can see them again.

At first there were all kinds of texts and calls from my friends. *I'm so sorry* and *Are you okay?* and *Do you need anything??* Invites to go to the movies, the beach, to this or that person's house for pizza and Mario Kart. I'd lie in my borrowed bed in my borrowed room, staring at the words on the phone screen.

Pizza? Movies? Who *cared*?

"Don't you want to see your friends?" the Andersons used to say to me. My foster parents were pretty people with pretty faces and pretty clothes and pretty little creases that formed between their eyebrows when they were particularly worried about me, which seemed to be all the time. They were nice, but in that surface-level way that made me think nothing really bad had ever happened to them.

I ignored the Andersons. Only left the house for visits with Kate and Zach. Left my friends on read. Eventually they stopped texting. When junior year started in the fall — only a couple of weeks after Zach's accident and Jack's emergency guardianship finally getting approved as a result — my old friend group had splintered apart. I steered clear of everyone, and they steered clear of me. Which was perfect. I didn't need anyone getting too close. Paying attention to me.

Liam's been a lot harder to shake.

"Sorry," I tell him. Below us, Kate and the other cheerleaders jump to their feet, spreading across the gym floor in perfect formation, pom-poms raised to the ceiling. Applause fills the air. "I'm not going to the game."

"Not going? To the biggest basketball game of the year that we'll definitely lose?" Liam grins. "Traitor."

I try not to smile back. But it's like trying to fight the pull of a really strong magnet. "I know. It's devastating. I may never recover."

The cheerleaders do a trick of some kind. There's another burst of applause. Liam has to raise his voice to be heard over the noise. "Family thing?"

"A match. In Sacramento. Gotta leave right after school."

Liam's whole expression brightens, like a lightbulb turning on. I remember Kate in the kitchen this morning. *You gonna see Pretty Boy today?*

"Nice," he says. "Who's favored? You or the other girl?"

I imagine whatever man I'll be paired against tonight. Taller than me, buffer than me.

"Definitely not me," I say.

"Oh, come on."

"How would you know?" I laugh. "You've never seen me fight."

"There's an easy solution to that."

I roll my eyes. "Yeah, okay."

"I mean it!" Liam leans forward. "C'mon, Bo. I'd be a pretty crappy friend if I never saw you box."

Friend? Since when does working on a class project with a guy for one semester make you friends?

I don't say that, though. He's only trying to be nice.

Still, the image flashes in my mind. Liam in the warehouse. Seeing Jack's temper. The sleazy comments. The betting. The rudimentary rules that barely keep the fighters from killing each other. The blood and bruises and broken bones. Me, often the only girl in the room. My opponents — grown men, not teenagers like he thinks. Not to mention me, in the ring …

One of the things that can disqualify you from becoming a legal guardian is a criminal record, especially for something violent, like fighting. If Liam knew what my "boxing match in Sacramento" really was, if he told anyone, even accidentally, or told his police dispatcher mom …

"It's not a good night." I say it too sharply. Wincing, I try again, softer. "Maybe another time."

A beat. Liam shifts, turning ever so slightly away from me, eyes suddenly fixated on the cheer routine below us. His pink cheeks are even pinker.

"Yeah, okay," he says. "Another time."

THREE

When I get home, the nerves set in.

My usual pre-fight nap? I toss and turn too much to get any sleep.

Dinner? The inside of my mouth feels like cardboard.

"What's wrong with you? Eat," Jack says, jabbing his fork at my mostly full plate.

"I'm not hungry." My mouth is so dry, I could barely get down my last bite of chicken. If I eat any more, I'm pretty sure I'll choke.

"You're no good to me if you faint in the middle of the fight. Here ..."

Jack passes me another piece of chicken, like that'll somehow change my appetite. But as he moves, his gaze latches onto Zach, sitting in the chair to his left.

Jack sits up. Like he's only just noticed Zach is here. "I thought you were sleeping over at a friend's tonight."

Zach hiccups. His knife and fork are frozen, suspended over his plate. He glances at me. "I can't. I feel sick."

"Again?" Jack says. Zach's been invited to three sleepovers this school year, but he always ends up feeling too "sick" to go. This one was at Austin's house, this kid Zach's known since he was two, so I thought, *maybe*.

But it's a fight night. I should've known better.

"C'mon, little man. Don't tell me you're afraid of a sleepover." Jack ruffles Zach's hair, and Zach jumps, dropping his fork. Jack doesn't seem to notice. "We really need to toughen you up!"

Our uncle laughs, loud enough that I almost miss Zach hiccuping again.

"He's just not feeling well," I say.

That gets me a level-four scowl. "I wasn't asking you. Why aren't you eating?"

"I'm not —"

"More quinoa, Jack?" Kate gets up from the table, taking Jack's plate without waiting for an answer.

In what I swear is a literal blink of an eye, she's got Jack a second plate of food, picked up Zach's dropped fork, and refilled everyone's water. She smiles.

Jack blinks. He leans back in his chair, scowl gone. He digs into his plate. "Well. Thank you, Kate. It's nice to have someone actually help around here."

Finally, at 10:30 p.m., it's time to get ready.

First, Jack and I prep the cutman supplies. Medic used to bring his own, but since we still don't know Tyler's backup plan, we need to be prepared. Then I grab my boxing clothes, roll them up as small as I can, and shove them into my purse, along with my mouth guard and hand wraps.

Last, I change into a plain, straight navy dress. Cheap sparkly earrings and matching necklace. It might look like I was going to a school dance if it weren't for the zip-up I pull on over the dress and the ugly black sneakers on my feet. But I have to wear them. The shoes won't fit in my purse, and Jack will already be bringing in my gloves and the cutman stuff.

Last, I sit on the floor in front of Kate's bed. She sits crossed-legged behind me to do my hair.

She's barely started when Zach wanders over.

"Can I help?" he asks.

"Trying to take my job? I see how it is," Kate jokes. But she makes room for him on the bed. Together, they comb out the tangles from my hair. Gather it into three bunches. French braid it, slowly, Kate quietly instructing Zach. Their fingers are gentle against my scalp.

"Are you ready?" Jack calls from the living room. His voice bites. "Time to go!"

"Be right there!"

I grab my things and say bye to Zach. He's already in his pajamas, reading, curled up under the blankets on my bed like it's his. The state has strict rules for legal guardians — siblings of different genders have to have separate bedrooms. But Zach sleeps here so often, it might as well be his room, too. And since Jack's guardianship became permanent six months ago and the monthly check-ins stopped, our social worker isn't around to notice.

"Don't wait up for me, all right?" I tell Zach, hugging him. "I'll see you tomorrow."

He hugs me back, his grip surprisingly tight. He hiccups.

"Do you *have* to go there again?" he whispers.

Zach doesn't know about the Plan, which means he doesn't know the real reason I fight. And I do my best to keep the details of the ring from him, the same way I try to hide any bruises I get from Jack. But it's hard when I come home bruised and bloody once a month. After my very first fight, I came home with a line of crooked stitches in my temple, dried blood on my chin, and bruises everywhere. Spent the weekend in bed, covering as much of my body as possible in ice packs and bags of frozen veggies.

After, Kate told me that Zach never left my side. I honestly don't remember. I drifted in and out of sleep for those two days, popping ibuprofen like candy, oblivious to everything except the exhaustion and my aching muscles — and the wad of cash clutched in my hand. I'd remember the money, and for a few seconds, the pain would vanish. We were $200 closer to freedom.

I tell Zach, "I told you. I'm doing this for a reason. A good reason. You have to trust me. Okay?"

"Any day now!" Jack shouts.

Kate follows me into the hall, and before I join Jack, she squeezes my hand.

"Good luck." She grins. "And kick butt."

Jack drives.

Away from the apartment, away from the corner of the little shopping district the gym sits on. The shopping district turns into sagging bungalows, into Victorians modeled after the ones across the bay in San Francisco, into lone apartment buildings that grow more and more sparse as we move west across the island. This late, the streets are empty except for the occasional miserable-looking dog walker. The fog rolling across the island from the bay makes everything beyond La Salida disappear — the Oakland Hills, San Francisco.

Like the only things that really exist are Jack and the car and the road.

The fights are held in a warehouse only ten minutes from Jack's gym, on the northwestern side of the island where the Naval Air Station is. Well, used to be. It got shut down in the eighties, but the old buildings and giant warehouses are still here because nobody has the money to fix them up or tear them down. The roads are full of potholes, and the painted traffic lanes are totally faded. No houses or apartments. No lampposts. No traffic lights. The one stop sign we pass has a giant dent right in the middle of the pole, like someone drove into it.

The warehouse itself is at the heart of the navy base. Jack pulls into the makeshift parking lot on a giant, empty stretch of concrete, joining a massive cluster of cars. As I climb out of the passenger seat, I swear the fog is thicker here. I can barely see the bay, even though we're parked only feet away from the fifteen-foot drop-off that leads to the water.

Jack grabs the cutman bag from the trunk and slings it over his shoulder. "Let's go."

Walking up, the most obvious thing about the warehouse is how big it is: a massive gray tin rectangle that used to house boats getting repaired. Long, thin windows stretch horizontally around the entire building near the roofline — way too high for anyone to look inside. The wall facing the water is lined with ancient loading doors made of wavy metal.

One of those doors is open, the thud of the bass booming out. Officially, the warehouse is a club. On the first floor, people dance and get plastered. But on the second floor, a bunch of men — plus me — fight, the noise muffled by the club music, the crowds hidden among everyone going in and out of the warehouse. I blend in in my plain dress and simple jewelry. No one gives me a second look.

At the door, the bouncer cards me. But it's only for show. The guy knows us. He barely glances at my driver's license before waving me inside.

As always, the club downstairs is packed. There's a line at the bathroom and an even longer line at the bar. In the center of the cavernous room, a mass of people jump in time with the beat. A DJ waves his arm along with them, his face in shadow. The air reeks of beer and perfume and salt from the bay.

At the bar, Jack uses whatever magic he possesses to maneuver around the line without anyone noticing. It wouldn't be out of place here — no matter how gross — to see a guy Jack's age with a girl my age. But if the first rule of fight club is not to talk about fight club, and the second rule is *not to talk about fight club*, then the third rule is not to attract attention. Ever. So I hover a few feet away from Jack, leaning against the wall and pretending to be busy on my phone while he orders two whiskeys.

"Something good," Jack adds. "Whatever you recommend."

The bartender hands a beer to someone else. "Top shelf okay?" he asks Jack.

"I can handle it."

The conversation is a code. Jack hands the bartender two fifties, the ring's entrance fee. The bartender hands Jack two identical drinks. I can't see them from here, but I know he passed him two small yellow ticket stubs, too, one pressed against each glass.

My uncle raises a glass in salute, then slips away from the bar.

I give him a minute before I follow.

On the other side of the dance floor, in the shadows behind the DJ table, there's a small, plain door with a sign taped to it: PRIVATE EVENT: INVITATION ONLY. A man in all black waits next to it, arms crossed. His biceps are bigger than my head.

"Think he'll talk today?" I ask Jack.

"Don't be smart." Jack shakes the man in black's hand, slipping the two tickets into his palm. No ticket, no entry. And the tickets are stamped with today's date — no double-dipping.

The man checks the tickets, then nods and opens the door for us.

Up a flight of stairs to a small landing, where there's another closed door and two more men waiting outside it. The one on the left claps Jack on the back when we arrive. The one on the right takes our phones — they aren't allowed in the room.

"Password?"

Even though the guys know us, the password is protocol. It changes every time, spread by word of mouth before each fight. The final piece of security.

Jack hands the guys the two whiskeys. He rarely drinks. Definitely not on a fight night.

"'The will must be stronger than the skill,'" he replies.

"Cheers." The man on the right raises his glass to Jack with one hand and opens the door with the other. "Have fun."

When we walk into the room, the first thing that hits me is the smell. Hard liquor and beer. Cigarettes and weed. Sweat. A dozen different colognes.

Then the sound. The bass from the club's speakers seeping through the floor. The clink of glasses. Shoes shuffling along the stone. Men (and a handful of women) talking, yelling, laughing.

A year ago, the noise alone would've raised the hairs on the back of my neck and made me want to run home. Not anymore. The buzz hums through the soles of my shoes. There's something . . . comforting about it. My shoulders relax. I stand a little straighter.

Maybe that's weird. I mean, pretty much everything in this place is illegal. Fighting in an unlicensed and unregulated fight. Fighting as a minor. Taking money for fighting, which is only allowed for pros. Even just being here watching an unlicensed fight is illegal. Not to mention the betting on the fights and the drugs and I don't even know what else happening on the sidelines.

Any of it could get me arrested. Any of it would for sure disqualify me from being Kate and Zach's legal guardian when I turn eighteen.

But becoming a legal guardian takes money. A lot. And only winning the tournament will get me what we need before my birthday. It's in June — a little more than four months away. And I've done the math a million times. Even if Kate gave me all her money from working part-time at Starbucks after school — a job she picked up to pay for cheer — even if Jack let me work part-time, too, it wouldn't be enough. This is the only way.

And . . . I don't know. At least Jack tries to keep his temper in check here. At least here, I can hit back.

"Hey, Psychic! What's up, man?"

As usual, as soon as we set foot in the room, Jack's immediately swarmed by guys who remember him from his own days fighting here a decade ago.

He was a big effing deal, your uncle, Tyler told me once. He's the only guy in the whole ring who knows Jack and I are related, and it's only because of how far back he and Jack go. *Three years of fighting here, and he only ever lost one fight. You know why we called him Psychic? Because it was like he already knew what hits they were gonna throw before they did. He was practically unhittable. Never seen anything like it. Could've gone pro, but he decided to open that gym instead.*

"I'm gonna change," I tell Jack. I'm standing right next to him, but I have to shout to be heard.

Jack waves me away, busy with his fans.

There's a pair of unisex bathrooms at the back of the room. The line's short, but the few men in it still do a double take when they see me. One eyes the hem of my dress. Another smiles at me, all teeth.

I yank the zipper up on my hoodie and sink back against the wall, hiding in the shadows as much as I can while I scope out the room.

The second floor is laid out like the club, with a long bar sprawling along the wall opposite the bathrooms. The ring is in the center of the room, right above the dance floor below. Instead of a DJ table, there's a rectangular table where Tyler and his cronies sit during the fights. Tiny dilapidated offices line the walls, their doors propped open as bookies take bets. The room is dim, the only source of light a cluster of pot lights shining directly over the ring.

Crap lighting or not, I can tell that even though it's early, even though most people don't show up till the heavyweight fighters go on later in the night, tonight's crowd is already big, filling most of the room.

Soon, they'll all be watching me.

In the bathroom, I change into my shorts and tank top and put my zip-up back on, pulling the zipper up to my chin and the hood over my head, hiding my long hair. Lots of guys here wear hoodies. It'll help me blend in. Or blend in better, anyway.

I find Jack at the far end of the bar, in our usual two seats that Boss, one of the bartenders, always saves for us. Without a word, Jack takes my purse, gives me some Tylenol — preventative, to help with pain and swelling — and hands me my gloves. They're MMA gloves, purple, like fingerless gloves if fingerless gloves were heavy and had a bunch of extra padding over the knuckles and around the wrist. Most people here use MMA gloves, even though the fighting is closer to boxing and the added padding in boxing gloves would give more protection. But boxing gloves are too bulky to sneak into the club without being seen. Plus, with less padding, MMA gloves are lighter. That makes it easier to hit hard and get a knockout faster.

"Lineup's posted," Jack tells me, gesturing to a chalkboard behind the bar. There are three columns, one for each weight class: light, middle, and heavy. In each column, sixteen pairs of names are listed. *Hitman vs. the Bull. Gladiator vs. Edge. Batman vs. Superman.* (I'm not kidding about that last one.) For anonymity, everyone here fights under a stage name. Everyone chooses their own name, which is how you end up with things like Bicep Billy.

My name is about halfway down the lightweight list. *Hook vs. the Butterfly.*

I rub my fingers along my sweaty palms. I've seen my name — the Butterfly — on this board nearly a dozen times before, but never with so many other names before and after it. And never during the tournament.

"Good placement," Jack adds, nodding. "Plenty of time to get ready. And we can scope out the competition for the next round."

If I make it that far.

"Well, well, look what the cat dragged in!"

A man struts toward us — as tall as Jack, slim as a cigarette, with wavy red-blond hair streaked with silver. He's grinning his biggest grin, the one that makes me think of those stock-photo lawyers on billboards. As usual, he's wearing a white button-down, sleeves pushed up to the elbows and top button undone, tucked into a pair of dark jeans.

Basically, he looks like he belongs in the club downstairs, or in some high-rise in the city doing something techy. Not like someone who'd spend his free time running an illegal fighting ring.

Jack laughs and stands up. He and Tyler clap each other on the back in that way men do.

"Hey, Butterfly." Tyler turns to me. His handshake is crushingly tight. "You're still letting this old guy drag you here, huh?"

"Gotta get car money somehow," I say. That's what Jack thinks I'm saving for. Like he always says, the best lies are a little bit true.

"Good girl." Tyler turns back to Jack. He glances around, then adds in a lower voice, "Shame about Medic."

"Idiot," Jack says. "Everything else fine?"

"Quiet as a church. They won't find anything. But even if they do, my guys will squash it."

"Good, good. Who did you get for us?"

Tyler points. "Over there. By the ropes. He's working in the first fight, but he'll come over after to talk with you."

I look where Tyler's pointing. Hovering by the ropes is a tall, skinny guy in a navy T-shirt and glasses. He's holding a ziplock full of medical supplies: bandages and cotton balls and water and an enswell, a cold metal tool used to reduce swelling. The same stuff in the bag currently slung over Jack's shoulder.

Still, I frown.

Jack's frowning, too, as he says what I'm thinking. "I've never seen him before."

"'Course you haven't," Tyler says. "He's new."

"You hired us a *newbie*?" I blurt.

Tyler gives me a look. "You don't have to say it like *that*."

You'll find cutmen at any legit boxing match. People whose job it is, during the breaks between rounds, to tend to a fighter's injuries so they're in better shape for the next round. Cutmen keep the boxers in good condition, which makes the fights last longer, which makes betting more interesting and increases the amount of money Tyler makes, which makes the pot in future fights higher. Plus, it's practical. Better for a cutman to deal with your beaten-up face than, say, an ER doctor who'd ask questions about what happened to you and how and where.

Here, having a cutman is a rule. No cutman? No fighting. No exceptions. Tyler's really strict about it. During the regular fights, he always pays a couple of cutmen to hang around and help any fighter who doesn't have one of their own. And during the tournament, you can't participate unless you hire your own cutman — though Tyler will use his contacts to help you find one, if needed.

Like he was supposed to do for me tonight.

"What about Golden?" Jack asks Tyler. "Healer? The Elixir?"

"Too busy with other fighters. Be realistic. It's a big night. They're all booked four times over. I had to get creative. Junior there has a strong medical background and loves boxing. He's practically made for this."

When Jack still fought — before he opened the gym, before Tyler took over the club and the ring from the last owner

— Tyler was Jack's cutman. The best. I'm told he could freeze a swelling eye in its tracks, stop a bleed with a brush of his finger. That's how he got his name here: Midas. Because it was as magical as turning something to gold. Jack's near-perfect record? It was Jack's talent, yeah, but it was Tyler's, too. No fighter can go that far without a great cutman.

Based on the way Jack's jaw is twitching right now, that history is the only thing keeping him from punching Tyler in the face.

"I don't care what he's made for," Jack says. "An amateur tonight is a no-go. She's dead in the water."

"Psychic! Let's not be dramatic. You want the Butterfly to fight, don't you? Besides, you trained her. *You* promised me she was ready for this. Where's your faith in her now?"

Tyler smiles at me. I glare back.

Tyler checks his watch. "Don't worry, Butterfly. I have total faith in your abilities. Now if you'll excuse me …"

Without another word, Tyler turns and disappears back into the crowd.

The moment he's out of sight, I slump against the bar. "I'm screwed."

"Of course you're not," my uncle snaps.

"You just said —"

"Shut up." Jack drums his fingers on the bar top. "We'll watch him during this first fight. If he doesn't seem up to the job, I'll put myself down as your cutman, and I'll give Tyler a piece of my mind after."

This isn't exactly a stellar backup plan. That first fight? The one where I came back all stitched up and swollen? None of Tyler's cutmen would work for me — they didn't take me seriously — so Jack had to do it. Let's just say it's *really* not his thing.

"You're fighting tonight," Jack continues, "and you're winning, you hear me? Now go warm up."

So I move to the edge of the room, out of the way, where some of the other fighters are warming up, too.

Jack only let me start fighting here six months ago, after six months of coming here most Friday nights to watch and study, after six months of early-morning training. Even then, he'd only let me fight once a month. ("You're still learning. And you need time to heal. The last thing we need is anyone at your school getting nosy.") So I haven't fought most of these guys before. But I still recognize all their faces. Gladiator. Lion's Roar. Thunder. Even Bicep Billy.

These aren't the random, half-drunk guys who usually show up here on a regular Friday night, pay the $50 buy-in and throw a few messy punches before passing out, or the friends who step into the ring on a dare. These are solid fighters. Guys who fight nearly every week, or who have been coming here for years.

And I'll have to get past all of them if I want the grand prize.

"Is that *the Butterfly*?"

I freeze in the middle of my jumping jacks. I recognize the voice before I see him. Rooster. My very first opponent.

Rooster cackles. "Don't tell me you're in the tournament. What, didn't get enough last time? Here for more?"

The other guys guffaw. Thunder's eyes linger on my chest. "I'll give her *more*."

I move as far away from them as I can get. I try to focus on my movements. Leg stretches and arm stretches, jumping jacks, light shadowboxing. Not on the creeps still laughing and leering at me. Not the memory of Tyler's smile or the minutes ticking down to midnight. Try not to think about Kate and Zach at home. Try not to imagine all the ways the newbie cutman could ruin this for me and wreck months of planning in one night —

The room erupts.

Cheering, applause, stomping. A bunch of the guys at the bar rush away, joining the crowd pressing in toward the ring, and in a second they're all chanting: *"Midas, Midas, Midas."*

In the middle of the ring, Midas/Tyler — smiling his biggest, sharpest smile yet — raises his hands.

Immediately, everyone goes quiet.

"Welcome, everyone! I'm so pleased you're here." He sounds like it's his birthday and he's just been given the greatest present on earth. "Tonight is a special night— the first night of our annual tournament!"

More cheers. Tyler lets it go for a moment before continuing. "Tournament fights will be held monthly. The final will be in May. And if that's not enough, don't worry, we'll still hold our regular fights every Friday as scheduled. Tonight's fighters have all been handpicked by me. These are our *best*, and they all want to win the $25,000 grand prize! You're really in for a show!

"Each round will be two minutes, followed by a minute break. A winner is declared after a knockout or a yield. And we want a good fight! Right? So no biting, spitting, excessive holding, tripping, kicking, wrestling, head butting, choking, or otherwise unsportsmanlike behavior. Every fighter must wear protective gloves and a mouth guard. Fighters must have a cutman and are allowed a coach if they want one, but no one else. Winners of tonight's fights will win $1,000 each and move on to the next round of the tournament, which will be held one month from now, on the last Friday in February.

"Finally, we'd like to remind everyone that what happens in this room —"

Most of us have heard Tyler's speech so many times by now that we have it memorized, so it's no surprise when the crowd finishes the sentence for him: "Stays in this room." It still creeps me out. Like, is this a boxing ring or a cult?

Everyone hollers and claps as Tyler takes his seat at the table next to the ring and the ref calls for the first two fighters, Hitman and the Bull. I've never fought either of them, but I've seen them around.

"Who's favored?" I ask Jack.

He points. "Blondie there. The Bull. Solid record. Eight and one."

I raise my eyebrows.

"Exactly," Jack says.

Standing at the edge of the ring, the ref pulls an ancient-looking stopwatch from his pocket. "Fighters ready?"

When they both nod, the ref says, "Three … two … one …" He presses the stopwatch. "Go."

It takes about twenty seconds for the Bull to break Hitman's nose. Blood gushes into his open mouth, down the front of his tank top.

Jack laughs. "See? Solid."

At the break, Hitman's cutman, Doc, does the best he can, but there's only so much you can do for a broken nose. Nose taped, cotton balls shoved up his nostrils, eyes already bruising, Hitman goes into round two looking ninety-five percent knocked out already. The Bull is practically laughing as the ref counts them in. The crowd hollers, a wave of noise egging him on.

At first, Hitman's slow. Too slow. None of his hits land. He takes one to the stomach, the head. Tyler's leaning forward, and the crowd's chanting, "Knockout, knockout, knockout —"

But then he gets lucky. His fist crashes squarely into the Bull's temple.

Immediately, there's blood everywhere. On the mat, on Hitman's glove, running down the Bull's face.

"Oh!" the crowd groans.

The ref calls the next break, and the Bull rushes to the edge of the ring, where he meets the newbie.

Newbie tries. He does. He has the same stuff Hitman's cutman used earlier. But I don't need to have Tyler's front row seat to see that this guy is moving way too slowly. Making dumb mistakes. Not applying enough pressure to the cut. Forgetting to use the enswell. Freaking giving him aspirin — I can see the color of the label even from here — which won't work for at least half an hour, so it won't do anything for the pain. Plus, it's a blood thinner, so when it does kick in, it'll only slow down clotting. That's Cutman 101 stuff. I could do better, and I got a C in bio last year.

Round three is a joke. With a bleed like that, the Bull can barely see. Almost the second the ref says, "Go," Hitman gets him in the stomach once, twice, three times, a volley, *boomboomboomboom.*

The Bull sways. Collapses knees first, clutching his stomach. The crowd counts, "One, two, three, four ..."

Boss the bartender drags a step stool out from under the bar and uses it to reach the chalkboard, circling Hitman's name before the ref calls it.

The room erupts in a mixture of cheers and grumbles. More than one unhappy face glances at the bookies' offices.

I can see one guy arguing with a bookie a few yards away. He won't get anywhere, but I can't blame him.

It shouldn't have gone that way. *Wouldn't* have gone that way, if that cutman hadn't messed up so badly.

Jack gets up. Goes to Tyler's table. I see them arguing.

When Jack returns, all he says is "I'll be your cutman tonight. We'll figure out the rest later."

I only nod. I don't trust myself to speak.

After that, everything goes too fast.

Second fight, an even match that ends in a seventh-round yield.

Third, another broken nose and blood.

Fourth, head butting — enough of it that one of the fighters gets disqualified.

Fifth, stone-cold knockout that gets the loudest cheer so far.

Sixth, a slow, boring fight, all defense, no action.

The seventh pair goes up, and I'm next. I remove my hoodie. Smear my cheeks, chin, and forehead with petroleum jelly to prevent cuts. Put my mouth guard in. Jack wraps my hands. It takes him twice as long as usual because my hands shake.

I'm putting my gloves on just as the ref's voice rings out:

"Hook and the Butterfly, please! Hook and the Butterfly ..."

Jack grabs my arm, pulling me through the crowd to the ring. All around me, people cheer and clap and stomp. I try not to look as nervous as I feel. Going into my very first tournament fight without a real cutman is one thing. But I think of Zach tonight, trying to keep me at home. How badly injured will I be when he sees me next? And for what, if I don't win? The Bull is way better than me, and look what happened to him —

I stop two feet from the ropes.

I can't do this.

Still gripping my arm, Jack hisses, "What are you doing?"

When I don't move, Jack glances at the ring — my opponent isn't there yet, either — and then wraps his arm around my shoulders, leaning in so no one else can hear.

"Bo, why am I hard on you?"

I take a deep breath. Repeat what he tells me before every fight, what he yelled my very first day of training with him, when I couldn't get a single thing right and burst into tears in the middle of the gym.

"Because I could be great," I say.

"Because you could be *great*." He speaks quietly, his eyes focused, his face set. For once, no part of him looks or sounds or feels angry. "So screw everything else. Go be great."

I nod.

Jack nudges me forward. I step under the ropes into the ring.

For a moment, as I move to the center, the room gets very quiet. Women compete in the regular fights sometimes, but there's never been a woman in the tournament before.

Two guys at the front of the crowd are whispering to each other, gaping openly at me. The loudest sound is the bass through the floor. The heat from the lights makes my skin prickle. I can hear myself breathing.

Then someone laughs. "Is this a joke?"

Another laugh. The sound doubles, triples, quadruples, echoing like the inside of a cave. More than one person wolf whistles.

"Take your top off!" a man yells.

My face burns. Opposite me, on the other side of the ropes, Tyler is watching me intently. He won't help. He didn't want to put me in the tournament in the first place. Jack had to talk him into it. I can feel everyone's eyes on me, piercing like a hundred knives, worse than any hit.

As if it wasn't bad enough, my opponent arrives, slinking under the ropes like oil. He's about my height, looks maybe ten pounds lighter than me and about five years older. I've never fought him, but I've seen him knock guys out cold.

He raises his eyebrows, taking in my purple gloves, my clothes. A smirk stretches across his face.

"You get lost looking for the bathroom, sweetheart?"

The laughter's so loud, it hurts my ears.

"Must have. You're way too beautiful to be in a place like this." Hook's smirk widens. His eyes rove down my body and up again. "Or to be here alone."

My skin crawls. I give the creep my best Jack-level death stare.

But Hook only laughs. "Don't worry. I could never hit a face that pretty."

Hook reaches like he's going to stroke my cheek. I knock his arm away.

"I'd like to see you try," I say.

He looks at his hand, then at me. "Excuse me?"

"I said I'd like to see you try," I repeat, louder. For the first time all day, my nerves are gone.

The ref sighs. "Fighters ready?"

Hook's eyes glitter. He raises his fists and nods.

I nod, too, glaring at Hook as I get into starting position: left foot forward, knees slightly bent. Fists up.

Be great.

The ref looks at his stopwatch. "Three … two … one …" *Click.* "Go!"

We move in, bouncing on the balls of our feet. My heartbeat is everywhere — fingertips, knees, ears, throat.

The world falls away.

Hook wastes no time. He moves in with his namesake: a hook that I duck, his fist sailing over my head. He jabs, I sidestep. Another jab, jab, uppercut, hook — sidestepped and leaned away and ducked. For now, I don't throw any of my own hits, only watch my opponent, letting him tire himself out and learning his weaknesses, staying out of his reach and moving fast, waiting for the right moment to strike. Like Psychic taught me, like Ali. *Float like a butterfly, sting like a bee. The hands can't hit what the eye can't see.*

Again, Hook swings, misses.

His stupid smirk slips.

I grin.

Hook follows me all around the ring. He throws punch after punch, and I duck and lean, sidestep, pivot. Blood thumps in my ears in time with my heartbeat. Every muscle in my body hums.

Nobody is laughing at me now.

Sweat shines on Hook's forehead. Another hook, and this time when I duck, I swing, too. *Crick*, my finger joints popping as my fist crashes into his stomach once, twice, his breath hissing between his teeth. I step back out of his reach, and he steps in, following, teeth bared. He swings again, lifting his guarding arm just enough that there's room for me to strike again, *whump, whump*. He grunts. I straighten. Out of the corner of my eye, a flash of movement. I try to backpedal, but —

THUNK.

Vision blurring. Brain rattling in my skull. I stay on my feet, but the petroleum jelly didn't work. My temple is wet where his hook finally landed. It's hard to get cut by MMA gloves, but not impossible. Not when the hit's powerful enough. Not when you're a bleeder, like I am. My eye burns, vision tinted red.

For a second it's my first fight all over again, skin blood-slick. I picture going back into the ring, falling, my knees on the mat for too long, and the ref's voice calling out, *the Butterfly yields.*

"End of round one," calls the ref. "Break. One minute."

I collapse, elbows on my knees, blinking blood out of my eye. I lick my lips. The corner of my mouth tastes like old metal, salt. I can hear someone laughing as they say, "I knew she'd be caught cold —"

A hand grabs my wrist, pulling me to the corner.

"Get over here," Jack hisses.

"I can't see." I'm remembering all these stories he's told me about fighters who got cuts like this one, who couldn't stop the bleeding and the blood seeped into their retina, stayed there for too long, and left them blind. Every story always sounded sort of fake, the kind of thing he'd make up to freak me out, but nothing about it feels fake now.

I blink. Blink. Blink. But the blood stays. Everything blurs. I picture coming home to Zach with my eye like this, and having to tell Kate, *I'm out of the tournament. We can't leave in June.*

Panic claws up my throat.

"Keep it together. That was only the first round," Jack says, rubbing a washcloth over my face, soaking up the blood. He dabs coagulant cream into the cut, then presses the cloth hard against the wound — the pressure makes my face screw up in pain — to try to stop the bleeding.

"Crap," Jack mutters.

"What?"

His fingers dig in. "Stupid thing won't clot …"

More blood trickles down my face. Jack swears. I imagine the ref's stopwatch, the seconds ticking down. If it doesn't stop soon, I can kiss that prize goodbye.

I forget to use his ring name. "Jack —"

"Shut up." Suddenly he removes one of his hands. "You! Go away. I told you we don't need … wait. Is that what I think it is?"

"Who are you talking to?"

But Jack doesn't answer, just lets go of me completely, and I'm left sitting there, bleeding, the *tick tick tick* of the stopwatch still looping through my brain.

Then a pair of hands touches my forehead. I flinch, but not because of the pain. I know what Jack's hands feel like — calloused and always hot. But these hands are smooth and cool. Not Jack's.

I try to see who it is, but my eye is watering so badly that all I can make out is the vague outline of whoever's crouched in front of me. A brief flash of yellow. A messy wave of hair.

"Hold still," Jack snaps from above me. "You're still in this. He's trying to distract you by being aggressive and going to the body, but he can't keep that up forever. Let him wear himself out … and stay out of his range as much as possible. Strike again only when the moment is right. One good hit, and he's on the floor. You know this."

As Jack talks, the hands that aren't his keep moving. They wipe the blood from my face. Dab a cold cream over the cut. Apply a bandage. No more blood leaks out.

No cutman I've ever had, not even Medic, has stopped a bleed this quickly.

"Seconds out," the ref calls.

"Be great," Jack says, and then he's turning me around and pushing me back into the ring.

"Three ... two ..."

With the cut bandaged now, the more I blink, the more my vision clears. Hook is already in stance, barely a scratch on him. My head throbs.

"... one ... go."

Like before, Hook comes in fast, swinging and swinging, his feet always moving as I duck and slip out of his reach, a weird kind of dance, moving forward and back and sideways, sidestepping and leaning and blocking all around the ring. Breath heavy in my ears. Sweat stinging my eyes.

Kick butt.

My back hits the ropes. Hook's fists fly. I duck and throw my arms up, shielding my head and my torso as much as I can, but too many, too fast, and no room to maneuver away. *Hfft, hffft,* the rush of air forced from my mouth every time one of his hits lands.

Behind me, someone in the audience laughs.

I push Hook's fists away. Sidestep around him, maneuvering back to the middle. He follows — a little slowly. His arms are lower, too, hanging closer to his hips, leaving his head wide open.

Float like a butterfly ...

I let him move in. Let him throw a jab-uppercut combo that I sidestep and dodge. His fists fly through the air, carried by pure momentum. He's within arm's reach, unguarded —

Whump. I get him in the jaw.

WHUMP. Then in the head. Square in the temple. Hard enough that I swear I see his eyes rattle in their sockets.

He hits the floor.

The ref counts to ten.

Hook stands, but it's too late.

... sting like a bee.

A sound like a *whoosh.* Like everyone gasps all at the same time.

The ref raises my arm. "The winner is ... the Butterfly!"

The room seems brighter than it did before, like someone turned more lights on. My head and stomach throb, but the pain's distant. Separate from me. The only thing that feels real is the ref's hand on my arm, and my pounding heart, and Jack, at the edge of the crowd, grinning like crazy.

I start to smile.

Then the booing starts.

There are some cheers, too, and some clapping. But mostly boos. Someone yells, "Oh, come on!" Someone else adds, "It's not fair!" A middle-aged man at the front of the crowd looks me right in the eye, then spits on the floor.

Quickly, I move out of the spotlight of the ring, back to the dim lighting in the crowd. Jack's right by the ropes, scowling at everyone around him.

"Sore losers," he says loudly. But then he grins at me. "What'd I tell you, huh, what'd I tell you?"

"Yeah." I remove my mouth guard and gloves — my hands immediately feel lighter — while keeping an eye on the man who spit at me. He's still glaring. "Can we go?"

"Hang on. You need to thank your cutman!" Jack grabs my shoulders, steering me so I'm facing someone standing behind him. Jack is so tall that I didn't see him before. "Offered to help after you got hit. He's new, but *worlds* better than that glasses kid Tyler tried to force on us. And he's got a real edge over the other cutmen ..."

I look, and the sound around me turns fuzzy, like an out-of-range radio station. I don't hear the rest of Jack's sentence, or the crowd, still grumbling over my win, or the ref, calling for the next pair of fighters.

I'm too focused on the figure in front of me.

Messy honey hair. Mouth open. Pink flush in his cheeks.

"Liam?"

FOUR

It's like he was transported here straight from the pep rally. Carhartt pants. Mills hoodie, navy and yellow. The only difference is now he's clutching a half-empty plastic water bottle, a small makeup-like tube, and Jack's cutman bag in his hands.

"What are you *doing* here?" I demand.

"What are *you* doing here?" Liam shoots back. But his tone is kind of canceled out by the fact that his face bypasses every shade of pink and goes straight to red. I didn't know it was physically possible for a person to blush that hard. Maybe he has a disease. Megablushingitis. He keeps glancing over his shoulder, shuffling his feet, like he's thinking about bolting.

Jack looks back and forth between us. "You two know each other?"

A guy standing behind Jack leans in, scowling. "Hey. Move this reunion somewhere else, will you? Some of us are trying to watch the fight."

"Screw you," Jack snaps, but he grabs my arm and gestures for Liam to follow.

Jack leads us to the edge of the room. It's even darker here, and nobody's nearby except a guy smoking a few feet away.

The lit end of the cigarette glows red-orange.

Jack jabs a finger at me. "Explain."

"We go to school together. We're in the same grade." I'm staring at Liam. *This can't be happening*. "But I don't understand, why are you ... how ..."

"There you are!"

Tyler appears, moving through the masses as easily as a bird through the air. A few people do double takes when he passes them. Usually he doesn't leave his table until the fights end.

I assumed Tyler was talking to Jack, or even to me. But instead, he makes a beeline for Liam.

Tyler wraps an arm around Liam's shoulders. He laughs. "Well, I wasn't expecting this!"

"I'm sorry," Liam says. "I —"

"Sorry! Don't be sorry. What you just did was incredible! How did you find us? And how'd you get *that*?"

He points to the makeup-like tube in Liam's hands, which Liam immediately gives to Tyler.

"You dropped it when you left." Liam's eyes move around the room. He shifts fractionally closer to Tyler. "I thought you might need it ..."

Now that Liam and Tyler are standing next to each other, the resemblance is obvious. The same high cheekbones. Same slim build. Same eyes and nose and honey-colored hair.

I rack my brain, mentally combing through hours of mock-trial prep with Liam in gov. I remember him mentioning his mom a few times, but not his dad.

But I think of how Liam's smile always seemed familiar to me, and I feel really, really stupid.

Jack's eyes move from Tyler to Liam and back again. "Midas. Is this ... your son?"

Tyler pockets the tube, practically bouncing. "A surprise appearance. But not as surprising as what I just watched!"

He turns his attention to me. "What a performance, Butterfly, what a show! A knockout in two rounds? *That's* why I do this. *That*'s a good fight. Well done. Here, come with me, let's get you paid."

Jack raises an eyebrow. Fighters and their coaches usually pick up winnings directly. Tyler never gets involved unless there's a dispute of some kind.

"You don't need to do that. The fights are still going on."

"Don't worry. It'd be my pleasure."

Keeping an arm firmly around Liam, Tyler leads us to the other side of the ring. We pass the line for the bathrooms and arrive at one of the offices along the wall. Tyler pulls a key from his pocket and unlocks the door. Inside, a pair of men sit at a table, locked cashboxes stored carefully behind them. Bookies operate out of the offices around the floor, but fighters' winnings can only be received from this room. The Treasury, it's called.

It's tiny. There isn't room for six people, so Tyler gestures for me and Liam to wait outside while he and Jack get my winnings.

The moment the door closes, Liam moves closer to me. Behind us, a kind of rumbling sound builds, the crowd getting riled up by whatever's happening in the ring.

"This place is *insane*," Liam says. "That fight — *all* the fights — the stuff those guys were saying about you ..." He shudders. "Bo, what are you *doing* here?"

"Shhhh! Don't use my real name."

"What does that mean? What else am I supposed to call you?"

I lean against the wall. I don't want to be having this conversation. The adrenaline from the fight's already wearing off, and my face is starting to throb.

"Liam, why are *you* here?"

He leans against the wall, too. "I asked you first."

"Well, I asked earlier, so I have dibs."

He sputters. "That's not how that works."

I smile. "Sure it is."

"You have to call it for dibs to count," Liam says. "You didn't call it. So, no dibs."

"Fine. But there's not much to tell." I gesture to the room. "Welcome to my boxing match in Sacramento."

"Ha, ha. I mean, like, how'd you end up fighting ... here?"

Every organ in my body ties itself in knots, remembering. What would I say, if I could tell him the truth?

It was a year ago. We'd been with Jack for six months. Kate and I had been researching everything we'd need for our new plan, legal fees and rent and a car. It was all so expensive. A part-time job was never going to get us the money in time. In the middle of the night I found myself downstairs in the gym, trying not to have a panic attack, trying to breathe. I started hitting one of the bags. Just hitting it, over and over and over. I don't know for how long. But when I finally stopped, I could breathe again, and Jack was there watching. I thought he'd be angry. Instead, he offered to train me. Said I was a natural, and with proper training, I could fight. Make money. Maybe a lot of it. Like he did when he still fought. I thought of Kate and Zach upstairs and it felt good, hitting the bag like that, and I thought, This is our way out —

I swallow. Choke the words back like a giant pill.

"I wanted to earn some money. My uncle thought I could fight." I shrug. "He used to fight here with your dad as his cutman. He trained me and brought me here." Technically, it's not even a lie.

Liam raises his eyebrows. "That's it?"

"That's it. Very boring." I point at him. "Your turn. Spill."

Liam glances at the Treasury door before answering. His voice is so low that I have to lean in to hear him over the crowd.

"I didn't know about this place until tonight. I swear. I only found out about it because I kind of … followed my dad here."

"That's it? That's all I get?"

"That's what happened."

I roll my eyes. "So, what, you want me to believe that your *dad* was running a fight club for, like, *years,* and you had *no idea*? Where'd you *think* he was going every Friday night?"

Behind us, the crowd groans.

"My parents split when I was six months old. I'm only at my dad's one weekend a month. He's a paramedic, and he's busy a lot. He told me he had the overnight shift on Friday nights. But I guess that was just a cover for coming here." Liam shrugs, but he taps his knuckle on the wall, staring at a gouge mark in the stone. "This is my weekend at my dad's. Tonight, he dropped the CutPro as he was leaving. I thought he was going to work and he'd need it, so I followed him here, and —"

The Treasury door opens. Jack and Tyler emerge, Jack zipping the cutman bag closed. It looks bulkier than before, and even with all the noise, I swear I hear him humming under his breath.

While Tyler locks the door, Jack turns to Liam, handing him a small wad of bills — Liam's cut of the prize money.

"You've really never done this before?" Jack asks. "Ever?"

Liam shakes his head. He pockets the cash without even counting it.

Jack grins at Tyler. "He's a natural."

"Of course he is! Takes after his old man." Tyler claps Liam on the back, making Liam grin wide enough that his eyes scrunch.

Tyler holds up the little tube Liam gave him earlier. "Good tools don't hurt, either."

Jack laughs. "No. They don't." He nudges me. "That's CutPro."

I raise my eyebrows. No wonder Liam could stop the bleed so fast. No wonder Jack said Liam has "a real edge."

CutPro is this hemostatic cream, designed to stop even severe bleeding in a few minutes or less. There are similar products available over the counter, and legit cutmen will use those, but they usually come in the form of big pieces of gauze, or even powder, which is trickier and slower to apply than a cream. CutPro is one of the few creams out there, and it's by far the best. At least, that's what Jack told me. I've never actually used it before tonight because only medical professionals like Tyler can purchase it. And I'm ninety-nine percent sure it isn't legal to use here, like this.

"You wouldn't be in the market to sell, would you?" Jack asks.

Tyler pockets the CutPro, roaring with laughter. "It's worth more than my job to sell you that. You know what I had to do to get this? Or what kind of trouble I'd be in if anyone found out I was using it outside of work?"

"What about a loan? A special arrangement ... for family?"

I frown. *Family?*

But Tyler only smiles.

Jack turns to Liam. "How about it, kid? We'll need someone for the rest of the tournament. You in?"

"What?" I sputter.

"What d'you say, son?" Tyler adds, putting his arm around Liam again. "We could use another cutman around here. Especially someone with natural talent like you! And I'll give you a leg up. You'll make a real splash with the CutPro. How'd you like to learn the family business?"

Liam looks at his dad. Glances out at the room. Back at his dad.

"I … I don't know."

Tyler blinks. "This is a very generous offer."

"I'm sorry, I wasn't trying to … I didn't expect … this is a lot, and I just wanted to talk to you about —"

The corners of Tyler's mouth seem to harden. "I already told you I misspoke."

"I know. But —"

Tyler removes his arm. "You don't want to? That's fine. I understand. Forget I asked. Not everyone can handle this place."

I wince. *Ouch.*

He laughs, clapping Liam on the shoulder again.

To me and Jack, Tyler adds, "Don't worry. Half the fighters here will be done after tonight. I'll get you a real cutman before February. Go on, Liam." He gestures to the door. "Go home."

There's a beat. I press the toe of my shoe into the floor, wishing I was anywhere but here.

"Yeah. Okay." Liam's face is an open wound. He glances at me. "See you Monday."

Liam leaves so fast, it's like I blink and he's gone, leaving me, Jack, and Tyler standing there.

"Well." Tyler claps his hands, all billboard smiles and white teeth again, like this wasn't the weirdest fifteen minutes of my life. "I'd better get back to my seat! Congratulations again, Butterfly. I look forward to your next fight."

After Tyler leaves, Jack and I head back to our seats at the bar. Jack's quiet, his eyes far away, jaw working. He smiles briefly at the bar top.

"What?" I ask.

"Quiet," he says. "I'm thinking."

What Jack's thinking about doesn't become clear until more than an hour later, when we walk into the apartment. We stayed through the rest of the lightweight fights so I could watch my competition. Usually, Jack makes us stay for the middleweight and heavyweight fights, too. To watch. Learn.

But not tonight. Jack spent the rest of the evening quiet, attention far away, then hopped up to leave the moment the last lightweight fight ended.

I figure maybe he's tired. Even dictators have to sleep. But before we go upstairs, Jack stops me.

"Here," he says. "Your cut."

I run my fingers over the corners of the bills, smiling. Four hundred dollars. It's double what I make at a regular fight. Double!

He laughs. "Exactly. And it's only the first round. Winnings go up every round you win. You know that, don't you?"

Of course I do. But there's something in Jack's voice that makes me look up.

"Listen," Jack says. "Give it the weekend. Let the kid cool down. But when you go back to school on Monday, I want you to talk to him. Convince him to be your cutman for the rest of the tournament."

"*Liam?* Why?"

"The CutPro, that's why. That bleed was going to take you out, and you know it. If you want to win this tournament, we need it. Besides, the kid's got raw talent. Couldn't you tell? Good tools or not, not everyone could do what he just did without any experience. With some training, he'll really be something. Think of the money! Think of what we could do!"

Jack laughs. Even in the dark, I can see the gleam in his eye — the huge, manic grin that seems to swallow the lower half of his face. He hasn't looked at me like that since that night a year ago, when he found me down here hitting the bag for the first time.

"You could be *great,* Bo," he says.

Can I? All I can think of are the many things that could go wrong. What if tonight was a fluke and Liam's not actually any good? What if Liam tells his mom about the ring? What if Jack loses his temper around Liam? Jack's never hurt me in public, but what if he gets mad, and Liam starts paying more attention, putting the pieces together?

No. It's too risky. All the cash in the world won't matter if this gets out at school and some teacher calls CPS and Kate, Zach, and I get separated again. Or if I get arrested for illegal fighting. I mentioned that to Kate once, and she was like, *You're a kid, they wouldn't arrest you.* Bull. Kids get arrested all the time. Tried as adults, even. And it's not like Jack's forcing me to fight.

Liam *cannot* be my cutman.

When I don't say anything, Jack's smile evaporates.

"What?" he snaps. "Spit it out."

"His mom is a police dispatcher!" I burst out. "What if she catches him sneaking out, or finds out what he's doing? And he goes to school with me. What if he tells someone?"

"Why would he do that?" Jack snorts. "He'd be putting his own dad in prison. You're not gonna tell. He's not gonna tell. And his mom is a dispatcher. Not a detective. You want to win, don't you?"

The cash crinkles in my hand. "Of course."

Jack flashes his teeth at me. "Then I don't see the problem."

I throw up my hands. "I don't *want* him."

"I didn't ask what you wanted!" Jack's yelling now. "I told you what you're doing!"

"I won't do it!"

SMACK.

The sound. Then the pain. Sharpest over my cheekbone, radiating beneath my eye and down to my jaw. Hard enough to make my eyes water and my left ear ring faintly.

I hold very, very still.

"I'm not," Jack repeats, "*asking*. You *will* talk to Liam on Monday. You *will* convince him to be your cutman."

His hand is still raised.

I whisper, "Yes."

FIVE

By the time I get into the apartment, to the bathroom, and close the door, my hands are shaking so badly, I can't even break one of the disposable ice packs I keep in the cupboard beneath the sink.

Smack. The memory of the sound reverberates in my head like it's happening again and again and again.

Deep breath in. Deep breath out. I wish my fight against Hook was now. I wish I had a do-over. Or that I was in the gym with one of the bags, hitting until the pain in my hands was stronger than the pain in my face.

Knock knock.

I jump about a foot and nearly drop the ice pack. But when I open the door, it's only Kate, wearing leaf-green pajamas and a smile. I can see her phone in her pants pocket, lighting up.

"You're back!" she whispers.

"Yeah." It's hard to focus on the conversation. I'm gripping the ice pack as tightly as I can to hide my shaking hands, but it still won't pop.

Keep it together. It's bad enough when Kate sees Jack hurt me. She doesn't need to know about the times she doesn't see, too. "Did I wake you up?"

"No. I was FaceTiming with Emmy and Maya and we lost track of time. We were supposed to be working on our project for AP Euro, but then Maya told us she wants to ask Mateo out, but Emmy and I agree, she's definitely *not* over Joy yet, so we told her — well, I'll tell you the rest tomorrow when you're more awake. Also, Zach fell asleep on your bed. Sorry. I swear, one second he was awake and then the next he was snoring — oh my gosh. I almost forgot! How'd the fight go? Did you kick butt?"

Almost *forgot?*

Pop.

The ice pack finally cracks. Cold rushes through it, chilling my hands.

The pain fades to the background. My hands are still, and that jittery feeling leaks away like water down a drain. My heartbeat slows.

"Yeah. I did." I wrap an arm around my sister, resting my head on hers, ignoring how raw and tender my cheek feels.

The next day, Jack fusses.

He lets me sleep till the afternoon. When he comes upstairs after teaching his usual Saturday morning sparring students, he spends forever drawing me a warm bath to relax my sore muscles. Gives Kate a break from cooking and makes me a big post-fight recovery brunch: oatmeal with blueberries and bananas, eggs and turkey bacon, a big stack of toast. He sits at the table with me, making sure I eat plenty and drink lots of water and take three Advil. Kate and Zach camp out in the living room. In Jack's sight, where he likes us, but also out of his way.

"Rest," Jack tells me, ushering me back to bed. "That's all you need to do today. Rest and recover." He hands me a fresh ice pack, and I have to clench every muscle in my body not to recoil away from him. He says nothing about my black eye.

It's a relief when he goes back to the gym.

I tell Kate and Zach I'm going back to bed. Then I lock myself in my room and get to work.

First, the Book. It's a plain composition notebook, something I found in a box marked FREE outside the school one afternoon. But I don't go anywhere without it, and at home, I always keep it zipped up in the laptop compartment of my backpack, out of sight.

I take a selfie of my black eye. Then I print it out on the cheap wireless photo printer I got at Walgreens, the only thing I've ever bought with my winnings. The picture it spits out is small, but clear and sharp, bringing out the colors on my skin: deep purple along the lower eyelid, tapering to blue and a faint red as the bruise spreads toward the cheekbone. Not good. But as I flip through the Book — past pages of other similar pictures — I'm almost relieved. If BuzzFeed did an article on my worst bruises, today's wouldn't even crack the top five.

I tape my newest picture on the next blank page in the Book. Beneath it, I write: *Saturday, January 27, about 2:15 a.m. One hit on the left cheek. Picture taken same day about 3:00 p.m.*

Next, I add last night's winnings to the shoebox I keep beneath a loose floorboard under my bed. I wanted to open a bank account, save the money there, but every bank on the island has a rule that minors can't withdraw funds without a parent's permission, which basically means all my money would be under Jack's control until I turned eighteen. So shoebox it is.

Then it's time for damage control / inventory. My body feels like it got left in the dryer on the heavy-duty setting. I'll need more Advil in a couple of hours. An ice bath, too, to keep my muscles from stiffening any more than they already have. Plus another warm bath tomorrow. But the visible damage isn't bad. Only the black eye and the cut above my eyebrow, which isn't too deep, though the wound needs to be cleaned again.

"Here." Kate finds me in the bathroom, wrestling with a nearly empty tube of Neosporin, the tap running while the water warms up. "Let me."

Slowly, she washes the wound with warm water, careful not to pull at the edges of the cut. Smooths antiseptic over the gash with the tip of her finger. She's so gentle that I barely feel it. I close my eyes and tilt my head forward almost without noticing it, leaning into the cold antiseptic and Kate's calm hands. There's no universe where I'd ever let her set foot in that warehouse. But if there was, she'd make a great cutwoman.

I open my eyes. Kate's still pressing the edges of the bandage down. I think of Liam standing over me last night, working on the same cut. My whole body tenses at the thought of seeing him on Monday. Him knowing that I fight in the ring is already too much of a risk. How can I possibly let him be my cutman?

"Does it hurt?" Kate asks.

I shake my head.

"Liar." She presses a Band-Aid over the cut. "Who cleaned

this up? Last night, I mean. It looks better than usual."

When I hesitate, Kate says, "Spill."

"Liam ..." I make a face. "Liam showed up at the warehouse. He was my cutman last night."

Kate's eyes bug out. *"Liam Covey is your cutman?"*

"Yes ... well, I mean, no, not yet ... it's complicated, okay?"

I fill her in on everything. My forehead bleed, the CutPro and Liam's miraculous cutman abilities, Tyler being Liam's dad, Jack making me promise to convince Liam to work for us. (I don't tell her how he made me promise.)

When I'm done, Kate's quiet for a second. Then, very seriously, she says, "You know Liam's hot, right?"

I whack her arm. "You're totally missing the point."

"Um, you're telling me that that Pretty Boy is gonna be spending a *lot* of time with you. How am I the one missing the point?"

I keep my mouth shut so I don't snap at her. How can she joke around? Doesn't she get what an impossible situation this is?

Finally, I say, "He'll only be spending time with me if I can convince him to come back."

"'If'? I told you he's obsessed with you. All you have to do is ask and he'll come running back." Kate sits back, admiring her handiwork. "Look at that. I'm almost as good as Liam. Ha! Hey, your cheek looks swollen. Do you want more ice?"

Last, I update the spreadsheet.

I don't get to it until evening, after accidentally falling asleep on the couch while icing my cheek. After dinner and another hot shower. After sitting at the foot of Zach's bed, reading *Percy Jackson* to him until he fell asleep.

I'm back in bed now, working on my phone. It's late, but

Kate's in the middle of the room, AirPods in, marking the choreography for a new cheer routine the team will be practicing on Monday. Jack went to bed ages ago; the gym opens at 6:00 a.m. on weekends, too.

I go to the "Savings" tab on the spreadsheet.

Needed Items & Estimated Costs

Used truck: $5,000

Rent: $2,000/month (x3 months)

Utilities: $150/month (x3 months)

Security deposit: $1,000

Groceries: $300/month (x3 months)

Gas: $150/month (x3 months)

Phones: $60 (x3 months) (could ditch, but not ideal)

Lawyer: $350/hour (have enough for 5 hours to start)

Car insurance: $450/month (x3 months)

Renter's insurance: $25/month (x3 months)

Furniture: $1,000 (whatever I can't get for free on Facebook Marketplace)

TOTAL NEEDED: minimum $18,155

The only number I touch is the one in the last row, which becomes: *TOTAL SAVED: $1,400*

I stare at the numbers like they'll magically switch. Like that money in the shoebox under my bed will multiply itself by sheer force of will.

I still need so. Much. *More.* And I only have four more months to get it.

Because this is the Plan:

In June, on my eighteenth birthday, right after graduation, I'll open a bank account and deposit all my winnings from the tournament and every dollar of my savings.

I'll buy my car.

I'll start the full-time job I'll have lined up by then.

I'll file an application for my own apartment.

And finally, I'll meet with the good but reasonably priced family law lawyer I'll have made an appointment with for that day. I'll tell them about Jack. Give them the Book as proof of everything I say. I'll ask to file emergency guardianship paperwork so Kate and Zach can live with me as soon as possible. My car, my apartment, my job, and my savings will be proof that I'm ready for this. I'll tell CPS about Jack, and after they investigate, he'll get arrested — the only thing that's guaranteed to keep him from somehow keeping guardianship of Kate and Zach. The only thing that will completely protect us from him. And then Kate and Zach and I will live far away from here. Together.

But I can't do any of it if I don't have enough money in June. There are programs from the state I can apply to for help with things like groceries, but I don't know how long it will take to be approved for those, and I don't want to risk anything. I'd rather have the money and not need it than the other way around. So I need to win the tournament. Get my share of that $25,000 grand prize, a whole $10,000 — not to mention the winnings from the other fights along the way. I've done the math. Forty percent of all the winnings will put me a couple of hundred dollars over my goal.

"Bo?"

A hiccup. Zach's in the doorway, book clutched to his chest, tears streaking his cheeks. The hallway behind him is pitch-black.

I sit up. Kate pulls her AirPods out.

"I had a ... *hic* ... bad dream," Zach says. "Can I sleep in here ... *hic* ... with you?"

He's never had nightmares back-to-back nights before.

I'm making room on the bed and reaching for Zach before

he's even finished the question. He curls up to me and I wrap my arms around him.

"Do you want to talk about it?"

I feel, rather than see, Zach shake his head. But he hiccups again. His fingers grip my arm.

"It's okay," I tell him. "You're okay. I've got you."

There isn't space, but Kate perches on the edge of the mattress anyway. She runs her fingers through Zach's hair. She looks at me, eyes wide, lost. Usually, she's asleep when Zach has nightmares. She isn't used to this.

Hiring Liam would be risky. But it *does* seem unlikely that he'd do or say anything that would get himself or his dad in trouble. And I've kept Jack's temper a secret all this time. Surely I can keep it hidden for a few more months.

And Jack's right about the CutPro. That cut last night would have taken me out. The competition's only going to get tougher, my opponents bigger and stronger and more skilled.

I reach over Zach and take Kate's hand.

"June," I mouth to her.

Sunday, January 28

9:41 a.m. Me: Hey

9:42 a.m. Liam: No.

9:43 a.m. Me: All I said was hey!

9:45 a.m. Liam: The last time you texted me was about our gov project last semester

9:46 a.m. Liam: I'm not doing it

9:46 a.m. Me: Where's your sense of adventure?

9:49 a.m. Liam: I won't tell anyone about you or your uncle. Promise. But I'm not going back there

9:52 a.m. Me: Hear me out. Please

10:17 a.m. Me: Liam?

Sometimes, if I'm still too sore, or if my injuries are too difficult to hide, Jack will call me in sick the Monday after a fight. Today's a day where I could justify that. The cut is right in the middle of my forehead, and my black eye is at the gross, intense purple-blue-black phase — the kind of mark that's going to get a lot of questions, even with my boxing cover story.

But after training I spend twenty minutes carefully erasing the bruise with makeup. Pull a beanie on to cover the cut, gloves to cover my swollen knuckles.

But gov is a semester class, so Liam and I don't have any classes together anymore. The only reason I know he's at school at all is a brief flash of his stupid messy-haired head bobbing in the crowd after first period, carried in the tide down the hallway.

I text him again, but he leaves me on read. At lunchtime I can't find him anywhere in the cafeteria. When the last bell rings, I don't even see him by his locker, which is only a few down from mine.

He can't keep this up forever. That's what I tell myself as I trudge outside to the bike racks alone. Kate has cheer practice. Today's rain ended about an hour ago, but the wind is still sharp, making my sore cheek throb.

"Bye, Liam!"

I wheel around. First I only see Aaron Davies, waving. And

then I see Liam. Clambering into this ugly, half-rusted, powder-blue pickup truck. Pulling out of his parking spot and joining the line of cars waiting to leave.

My bike crashes to the ground as I take off, slipping across the wet sidewalk between clusters of students and teachers, ignoring a guy from my math class who flips me off as I dart in front of his car and narrowly avoid getting hit.

I don't realize how borderline crazy I'm acting until I skid to a stop next to Liam's car and knock on the passenger window.

Liam jumps about a foot. I can hear him swearing.

He rolls down the window. It takes a second because the car's old and he has to use a hand crank.

"What was *that*?"

"Sorry." My fingers dig into the little groove running the length of the passenger window. "But we have to talk about this."

"I already told you, I'm not … oh, ha, ha."

The last part is because I open the door and get into the passenger seat.

"You can't just get in other people's cars like that," he protests.

"You're the one who left the door unlocked."

BEEEEEEP. The car behind us lays on the horn, urging us to move up. I cross my arms and lean back.

Liam looks at me. His eyes move from my beanie-covered forehead to my gloved knuckles. Snag on my cheekbone.

"Geez," he says. "Did you get a black eye, too?"

I tense. "Yeah. Hook's volley in round two. Remember?" None of those hits were enough to bruise. Or anywhere near my cheekbone. But Hook was moving fast. Liam wouldn't have been able to see the volley well enough to know that.

I hope.

Liam looks at me for another moment. Slowly, he eases the car forward.

"I told you," he says. "I'm not going back there."

"Why not?"

"Because that place is crazy! Do you know how *illegal* everything in there is, Bo? Do you realize the trouble we'd be in if anyone ever caught us? We could kiss college goodbye for sure. I'd never be a doctor. My mom would *kill* me. And d'you know how long my dad would spend in prison if the police . . ."

Liam shudders. Outside, the wind picks up again, whistling, tapping on the windows like knuckles.

"Look," I say. "I can't fight without a cutman, and I need one. A good one. And I need the CutPro. You are literally the only cutman on the island who can get that for me. So —"

Liam snorts. "Wow, thanks. That doesn't make me feel used at all."

"It'd be great experience for med school."

"I can't exactly put *fight club cutman* on my application."

"There's money."

"You mean the fifty bucks Jack gave me? I could make more working at McDonald's."

"It's still money! And my uncle would train you, tell you everything you need to know. You might even like it —"

"*Like* it?" he sputters. "Yeah. Sure. Why are you even arguing with me about this? I saw your face when your uncle asked me to stay. You don't want me there."

I have to grip the door handle to keep from touching my bruised cheek.

Convince him.

"Do it for your dad."

Liam looks at me. The car behind us honks and dramatically

pulls around us to exit the parking lot. Other cars follow, but Liam doesn't seem to notice. He knocks the heel of his hand against the edge of the steering wheel.

"You heard him." His voice is raw. "He doesn't want me there anymore. Even if I wanted to say yes, I missed my chance."

I choose my next words carefully. "I don't know, like, exactly what's going on with you and your dad. That's none of my business. And I don't know why he got all weird at the end and asked you to leave. He was probably stressed. Or just bummed you didn't say yes right away. But, like, of course he still wants you there. *He* asked *you* to stay. He said you were *good*. And you are! I've never had someone stop a bleed like that. My uncle says, with some training, you could be even better than your dad. And nobody impresses my uncle, okay? And ..."

I hesitate. All weekend, I thought about Liam saying he only saw his dad one weekend a month. Pictured his excited face when his dad called him during the pep rally. Saw him moving closer to his dad after the fight, and his devastated look when Tyler kicked him out.

If Liam were my opponent in the ring, this would be where I'd go for the knockout.

"And ... I get it," I say. "About ... about having family you aren't with." I see the social worker's little blue car driving away with Kate and Zach. See my bed at the Andersons'. "Family you *want* to be with. Think of all the time you'd get to spend with your dad if you did this."

Liam looks at me, a crease between his eyebrows.

I hold my breath.

BEEEEEEEEEEEEEEEEEEP.

We both jump.

"I'm sorry, Bo." But not sorry enough to stop him from reaching across me and pushing the passenger door open. "See you around."

Panic flutters behind my ribs, the kind I feel when I'm in the ring, backed against the ropes.

I close the door again. Unbuckle and scoot forward as far as I can in my seat, leaning over the gear shift, blocking Liam from opening the door again. I'm close enough to see that he has a smattering of freckles beneath his right eye.

"Look. I stand by everything I said — about the money, and you being good at this, and about your dad. But, like, forgetting about all that, forgetting about how insane this is — I know it's insane — I just really, *really* need your help." I don't try to hide the tremor in my voice. "I *need* this money, I need to win this thing, and I have a way better shot if you help, and, just … you'd really be helping me out, okay?"

Liam's face twists. "Bo, I want to help you, but this is … if it was, like, *anything* else …"

Kate's voice echoes in my mind. *You know he's obsessed with you, right?*

Carefully, I touch his wrist.

"*Please*, Liam."

Liam Covey goes quiet. He looks up at me, eyes wide and unblinking, cheeks deep pink. He looks down at my hand on his wrist. Swallows. I can feel his pulse thrumming through his skin.

I fight the urge to squirm.

Whatever it takes.

Liam squeezes his eyes shut.

"When's the next fight?"

SIX

BANG.

"Ooooooh!"

The crowd around the ring cheers and shouts and groans as Strike steps away from me, his fists still raised. He rolls his shoulders back and cracks his neck, practically laughing as he bounces on the balls of his feet. His whole body is loose. Relaxed.

Tonight's opponent is my height but only five pounds lighter, thickly muscled. I'm feeling every ounce of that strength and weight right now. My head pounds. Literally. *Thumpthumpthump*, like a hammer knocking against my head where he hit me.

Someone in the crowd shouts his name. Strike raises an arm in response, leaving his side wide open. I move in —

The ref calls for the break.

Strike brushes past me, laughing.

"Don't worry," he says. "You can go home after the next round."

By the time I get to the corner, my forehead is already swelling.

"Okay, kid," Jack says, hovering as close to Liam as he can get. "You know what to do."

Looking faintly sick, Liam nods, fumbling to open the cutman bag and get the enswell.

Bad. He should already have the bag open, be ready to move when I get here.

"Ow!" I say, as Liam pushes the cold enswell against the lump on my head, right above my eye, like he's trying to flatten it.

His face turns pink. He eases up. "Sorry! Sorry."

I do my best to swallow my impatience. "Relax."

Liam gives me a very Liam-y version of a withering look—an expression I've gotten way too used to lately.

It's been a month since he agreed to be my cutman. A month of pretending everything is business as usual at school, aka never speaking to him except for an occasional "Hi" in the hallway. A month of Kate asking me every night before bed, "How was Pretty Boy today?" and Zach asking, "Who's Pretty Boy?" A month of me and Jack meeting Liam here every Friday night to watch the regular fights together. There's only so much you can do to train a cutman without actually putting him in the ring—Jack would never put me in another fight so close to the next round of the tournament—but we did our best. Watched the cutmen work between rounds, studying and critiquing them. Ran drills to help him memorize what's in the cutman bag and where so he can move faster during the fight. Ran through potential injuries and treatment plans. ("She's got a swollen eye and a lip bleed and took a hit to the head. What do you do?")

But training like that can only get you so far. The real test is tonight, now—the second fight of the tournament. The first fight I've had since we hired Liam.

Liam shifts the position of the enswell, fumbles, and drops it. He dives after it.

"Keep it together," Jack snaps.

Liam straightens, his red face glowing more brightly. He glances at the table where his dad sits, then back to me. "Sorry."

"He's trying," I tell Jack before he can say anything worse. The last thing I need is for Jack to get worked up in front of Liam. "Cut him some slack."

"'Slack' is going to cost us the tournament. C'mon, kid. Reduce the swelling. She can't go back out with that."

Liam tries. But he isn't the mysterious newbie who so miraculously fixed me up last time. His hands are shaky, his movements too slow. When the ref calls me back in, the swelling is a little better, but not much. It presses on the space between my eyebrow and my eye, bears down on my skull.

"Go."

Like Hook, Strike is arrogant and freaking annoying. But unlike Hook, he isn't sloppy, isn't wild with his punches. I bounce around the edge of the ring, staying out of his reach as much as possible. I don't want to get hit in the head again. He stays in the middle, turning with me, following my every move, but never moving himself.

We'll spend forever like this unless one of us does something, and my vision is only getting worse as the swelling intensifies.

When the ref calls the next break, I've barely hit Strike at all, but my cheek is bleeding, my fists hurt, and the swelling on my forehead is so bad, it's like trying to fight with a bag of marbles sitting above my eye. My vision is blurry, out of focus.

"Fix the swelling," Jack tells Liam.

"But the bleed —"

"She can't hit him if she can't see."

"Right. Right," Liam says, fumbling again for the enswell, and I could throttle him. He *knows* this.

"And you," Jack says, turning his attention to me. "What have I told you? Float and sting. Float and sting! Don't get into a tangle like that again if you don't have to, he's too close to your weight. One bad hit and you're gone."

Liam bends low, holding up the enswell. He glances at his dad again. Tyler's face is a mask, but he's leaning forward, neck angled toward Liam. He was all excited when Liam first returned to the ring. Smiling and joking. Giving Liam tips. Lending him the CutPro. But what if Liam chokes tonight?

I'm not gonna wait to find out. Tonight's prize is $2,500. I'm not losing my cut of that — or getting kicked out of the tournament — because of Liam.

He's still bent over me. I angle my face away from Tyler's view.

"Swelling," I mutter.

Only Liam is close enough to hear me. "What?"

"Fix the swelling," I repeat. "Now."

He presses the enswell to my forehead.

"Clean up the blood."

He does.

"CutPro," I say, but he's already reaching for the tube, loosening the top with one hand, applying it to my head.

"He dropped his left arm when he swung," Liam says suddenly. "I only saw it once, but maybe —"

"Seconds out," the ref calls.

Liam steps away. I blink. The swelling isn't much better, but it's not worse, either.

"Thanks."

Round three. My sight's still off, but I do my best to ignore it. I stay out of Strike's reach, waiting, waiting …

He comes in with two jabs, quick. I sidestep. He bounces away, then in again, hooks and uppercuts. I lean away and backpedal, watching, looking for an in. He swings with his right, his left arm dropping as he moves. Just like Liam said.

I catch Strike in the chin. Not hard enough that he falls, but enough that he grunts.

In round four, I get him again — twice in the chin and three times in the ribs, and his knees hit the mat. He stands up right away, jaw clenched …

By round five, Strike is snarling. He moves in fast, and we are a tangle of fists in the center of the ring, everyone around us hollering, jabs and hooks and jabs and hooks, *whump-whumpwhump* and knuckles crackling, grunts of air.

At the break, I leave with a split lip and my forehead swelling again, throbbing from a second hit in the same spot.

But by then, Liam's in the zone. He wipes the blood from my mouth, then presses a cloth to the cut to stem the bleed with one hand — it's not a bad enough bleed to need the CutPro — and holds the enswell to my swollen forehead with the other. The pressure is better. Liam's face is still pink, and he keeps exhaling loudly, like he's having to remind himself to breathe. But his eyes are focused, his movements steady.

When I stand up again and touch my eye, it's barely swollen.

Jack grins.

The ref counts us back in for round six. The crowd stirs, restless. The fights don't usually last this long.

Strike barely waits for "Go" before he moves in with a yell, the crowd roaring. I'm dodging, pivoting. Can't hit him again.

Can't even try, can't even take a second to think because he won't *stop moving*, teeth bared, eyebrows low, grunting with every attempted hit.

My back hits the ropes. He keeps swinging. I'm trapped, blocking and blocking, unable to move out of reach, using too much energy defending myself to try to hit back.

Some of my panic must show because Strike is smirking again. I have to hit him soon. I have to end this.

I swing under, aiming for his side because it's all I can reach. *Thumpthumpthump*, jab-hook-jab, and an uppercut to the chin —

He stumbles, enough that his knees hit the ground for the second time. The crowd roars.

In a moment, Strike is on his feet again, his face hard. His guard is down. I move in again.

He grabs my right fist just before it collides with his jaw. I try to pull my hand away, but he only holds on tighter, buckling the fabric of my gloves, his fingers pressing into my joints. Our fists are held low between our bodies, out of sight of the crowd.

No excessive holding.

Strike squeezes.

Hard.

Poppop.

Something moves out of place in the joints connecting my index and middle fingers to my left hand. I groan into my lips, pressing them together, shaking from trying not to cry out. Tears sting my eyes as I stumble back, cradling my hand to my chest.

Noise all around me. Shouting. Boos and cheers. All of it's too loud. The pain in my hand feels like its own kind of noise, somehow. Strike's openly laughing at me, turning to the crowd, pumping his fists in the air. The ref is still watching his timer.

The crowd rustles and stirs.

"She can't fight like that!"

"It's over! Call it!"

"He should be disqualified!"

The ref glances at Tyler. Tyler looks at the ref, his face impassive. The ref seems at a loss, but he keeps watching the timer.

Strike laughs and laughs and laughs. His arms are down, fists at his hips.

I smash my uninjured fist into his jaw.

CRACK.

Strike howls. The ref rushes over and examines him. Strike tries to push him away, but the ref shakes his head.

"Strike yields," he announces. "The Butterfly wins!"

The crowd erupts. The ref shoos a snarling, swearing, howling Strike away. I barely hear it. My eye and stomach throb where he hit me, the pain pulsing like a second heartbeat. And my hand feels like someone's jabbing glass into my joints every time my fingers twitch. I can't get my glove and hand wrap off fast enough, but when I do, I almost wish I'd left them on because it only makes the pain sharper.

But beneath that, my body hums, too. Part of me wants to go another round.

Jack pulls me out of the ring, arm wrapped protectively around my shoulders. Liam looks sick, but Jack's face is a lightning storm.

"Bastard," he snarls. "If Tyler doesn't ban that guy, I'll find him myself and —"

As if summoned by the mention of his name, Tyler materializes next to Jack. "Let's look at that over here."

Tyler leads us away from the ring. The crowd parts for him like the Red Sea. There's definitely more people here now than there were when I started. Some give me death glares when I pass. One guy tries to give me his phone number. Another brushes his hand on my hip, making me flinch and bump into Liam.

But some just ... let me walk by. One guy even nods at me.

"... took it like a man ..."

"... tough little thing ..."

Tyler and Jack usher me into the supply room. Messy shelves of headgear and gloves line the walls, along with containers of disinfecting wipes, hand sanitizer, and a couple of ancient-looking first aid kits. The sweat-and-weed stench is especially pungent, but now with the bonus scent of Lysol.

Liam starts coughing the moment we walk in and makes a face when Tyler asks him to close the door.

"Let me see," Midas says, crouching next to me. If a fighter gets a bad injury, he'll personally assess them, decide if it's something he can fix himself or if they should go to the hospital, which everyone tries to avoid at all costs.

Carefully, Tyler takes my wrist and peers at my index and middle fingers. They're both bent at the base knuckle, pointed sideways while the rest of my fingers are straight. Like two bent twigs.

Looking at it makes my head spin. But Tyler only smiles. "Just a dislocation! Good. I can fix this."

He grabs one of the first aid kits and rummages around before handing me an ice pack.

"Get that on your hand. We want to get the swelling down before I reset those fingers. Jack, come with me. We'll get your winnings. Oh —" Tyler pauses, hand on the door. "Well done tonight, Ace."

It takes me a second to figure out he's talking to Liam.

"Ace?" Liam asks.

Tyler grins. "You need a nickname if you're going to be a regular around here. Which I hope you will be."

Liam beams. It's the kind of smile that makes you forget there's only one dim lightbulb in the room. "Thanks, Dad. I mean, Midas."

The door closes, leaving me and Liam alone.

Before I can do anything with the ice pack, Liam takes it from me. He's grinning.

"I can do it," I say, but he holds it above his head, out of my reach.

"Isn't this kind of my job?"

As Liam lays the ice pack over my fingers, I try not to look at them, at the nauseating angle they're bent at.

"You okay?" Liam asks.

He doesn't mean to, but the ice pack shifts slightly in his hand when he speaks. Pain shoots up my hand, my arm. Tears sting my eyes.

"Amazing," I grunt, blinking.

We fall silent. The cold from the ice pack stings my skin a little, and I'm weirdly aware of the slight pressure where Liam's fingers hold the pack in place. Even if I didn't have two dislocated fingers, this would be weird. I don't know where to look. Or what to do with my hands. I draw my knees to my chest, then straighten them again.

"Sorry I kind of fell apart back there," Liam says suddenly.

"It's okay," I say, relieved to have a distraction from the weirdness and the pain.

"It isn't. I could've cost you the fight."

I don't know what to say to that, so I don't say anything.

Liam clears his throat. "Well. Thank you for, you know. Helping me. And you were really good. You know. Out there."

"Oh. Um. Thanks. You helped me, too. Noticing his arm dropping. That was good."

Liam shrugs.

"Really," I say. "Most people don't notice stuff like that unless they know the sport super well."

"Oh. Well." A corner of his mouth lifts. "Got a good eye, I guess."

"Yeah, you really — *ow!*"

A new wave of pain shoots up my fingers. I squeeze my eyes shut. I hear Liam shift, feel the weight of the ice pack move slightly.

"What can I do?"

"Distract me."

"Okay. Um. How long have you been fighting?"

"A year since I started training." Surely it can't hurt to tell him that. "But six months here in the ring."

"Why?"

I draw my knees up again. "I told you. Money."

"You could work at Starbucks or Safeway like everyone else."

I think of how I felt the first time I hit the punching bag. The feeling of a combo executed well, or moving around the ring, the rush of a win.

But to Liam, all I say is "They don't pay as well."

He hums, agreeing. "College money?"

Again, I hesitate.

"A car," I say. Then, when Liam looks like he's going to ask another question, I quickly add, "And my own apartment.

For after graduation. Maybe college later. I can't leave Kate and Zach right now."

"Zach?"

"My brother. He's still in elementary school. It's been really hard on him ... you know, everything ..." I don't have to say more. Dad dying and Mom leaving was the kind of news I never had to tell people. The whole island seemed to just know. "So I can't just ..."

I realize how closely Liam is watching me and shut up.

"How's ... um ... your mom?" I wince the moment I ask it. *How's your mom?* Really?

A pause. "If you're asking if she knows about the ring, she doesn't. She's been working nights. Didn't even know I was gone."

I shift slightly. "So with your dad ... he'd tell you he was going to work and then leave you home alone all night? Every weekend? Like, every weekend you were at his place, I mean?"

Liam shakes his head. "My mom would've gotten the custody agreement changed like *that* if he'd been leaving me home alone overnight every month. It didn't start till I was twelve. And he'd just gotten married, so my stepmom was around to watch me."

"You have a stepmom?"

"Yeah. And two half-sisters. They're four and two."

I try to wrap my head around the idea of Tyler having toddlers. "Does your stepmom know about ... all this?"

"I think so? I don't know ..."

I pause. "The last fight. You said your dad dropped the CutPro while he was leaving, right? And you followed him to return it because you thought he needed it for work? But then you ended up here instead."

"Yeah."

"And so then you, what, hung around the club until you figured out how to get upstairs?"

The tops of Liam's ears are pink. "Yeah."

"Why didn't you just go home?"

"I don't know." But Liam's fingers are still balled in his sweatshirt sleeves. He's staring somewhere past me, his eyebrows low.

"C'mon." I knock my knuckle against Liam's wrist, *tap, tap.* "I can keep a secret."

He lets out a breath — half exhale, half laugh. "It's nothing. Dumb stuff."

A burst of noise from the main room, quickly stifled as Jack and Tyler return and they close the door again. Jack practically bounces over to me and Liam.

"Happy payday! For you —" He hands Liam a decent wad of bills. "And for you."

The stack he gives me makes Liam's cut look like pennies. I do my best to quickly count it with one hand — $1,000, which puts my total savings at $2,400.

"I told you, didn't I?" Jack says, pocketing his own cut. "This is the dream team!"

He claps both me and Liam on the back. Not hard enough to hurt, but still enough that I flinch instinctively. Oh, crap. Did Liam notice?

No. He's watching his dad, not paying me any attention at all.

"Give the dream team a little breathing room," Tyler says, laughing. "I've got a couple of fingers to put back in place."

Jack gets out of the way, and Tyler crouches in front of me. I miss the ice pack the moment he removes it.

"This'll be quick. But it'll hurt," he warns.

"It already hurts," I reply.

"Whoa whoa whoa," Liam says. "You're just gonna reset it? Here?"

"She can't go to a hospital," Tyler replies, like it should be obvious. "Too many questions."

"What about Strike?"

"His jaw's broken. I can't fix that. I *can* fix this."

Tyler grabs my wrist with his left hand and my fingers with his right.

"Brace yourself."

I've barely tensed my shoulders when he wrenches my fingers back into place with a *snap.*

"Son of a —" I slam the ground with my other fist. My eyes water like crazy. "Holy crap. Holy *crap*."

Jack claps me on the back again.

"I did tell you it would hurt." Tyler takes an ACE bandage from the first aid kit and wraps my fingers together so quickly, I barely see him move. "Go straight home. Keep this on and those joints in place. Try not to move them too much. Ice that for fifteen minutes tonight, then for fifteen minutes every hour all weekend. And be careful the next two weeks, all right? You don't want them popping out of place."

"Two *weeks*?" I groan, holding my sore hand to my chest. Jack usually takes it (relatively) easy on me the first few days after a match, but I need to start sparring again in a week if I want to keep my training up for the next fight, only a month away. It's not a long time to train, but it's still long enough that I'll get out of shape if I'm not careful.

"Tough luck, Butterfly," Tyler says, putting the first aid kit back on the shelf. "It happens to the best of us."

"'Tough luck'?" Jack suddenly straightens. "That moron should be banned."

Tyler sighs. "Psychic . . ."

"What happened to 'no unnecessary holding'? 'No unsportsmanlike behavior'? Anyone else pulled that, and they would've been disqualified immediately. What was that?"

Jack's a little too close to Tyler's face. His hands are twitching, fingers curling in.

"Your uncle's kind of intense, huh?"

Liam says it innocently enough. But I'm watching him watch Jack. Replaying Jack snapping at Liam during the fight. There's a ringing in my ears like the practice tsunami warning alarm the island plays when it's running emergency preparedness drills.

Got a good eye, I guess.

A sudden, sharp pain in my right hand. I was gripping my knees, bending my fingers too much.

"Argh!" I'm not faking the pain or the yelp.

Liam immediately turns away from Jack, waving his dad over. Behind them, I watch Jack pace the width of the little room, hands still flexing at his sides.

We watch only through the rest of the lightweights. Jack would stay longer, but the pain in my fingers is too bad to ignore, even with the ice pack and the Tylenol in my system. Liam leaves with us. I tell myself it's a coincidence, that he's not still watching Jack or keeping an eye on me.

Jack and I arrive at our car, and Liam keeps walking. He's a few yards away when Jack's phone rings.

Immediately, Jack picks up. Faintly, I hear a voice on the other end of the line, but Jack moves away, out of earshot.

I stand by the passenger door, shivering even as the ice pack gets less and less cold. In the distance, I hear the rumble of a car engine start up, then fade away.

Finally, Jack returns. He unlocks the car without saying anything or getting in and immediately turns back to his phone, thumbs flying.

I can't stand it. "Who was that?"

"Don't be nosy. Get in the car."

But he's grinning at his phone screen as he types, his face alight.

SEVEN

Jack's lost it.

I mean, like, more than usual. For the next month, he's always on the phone. Always … *smiley*. And once my fingers are fully healed, he's got me training like crazy. Longer runs. More weight training. Sparring with him nearly every day. I'm lucky if I'm able to stay awake past 9:00 p.m.

"Making sure you're ready," he replies when I ask him about the training ramp-up halfway through a particularly brutal set of burpees. We're a week out from the third tournament fight. There's a glint in his eye that reminds me of the nature documentaries my environmental science teacher makes us watch: the gleam of a jaguar's fur in the trees; the flash of a snake's scales, barely visible in the grass. "Making you *great*. Now run it again."

"It's like we're going to the Olympics or something," I complain to Kate as we stand side by side at the sink that morning, rinsing dishes. "I want to win, too, but, like, overtraining is just as bad as undertraining. And why's he on the phone all the time? It's not like the gym's that popular."

"Maybe he's got a girlfriend," Kate says, loading a plate in the dishwasher. "Or a boyfriend. Hey, do you wanna watch *Love Island* tonight? All my friends are having a watch party at Emmy's, and I'm the only one who can't go."

"Actually, I was thinking that if Jack's working late again, we could —" I double check that Zach's out of earshot. "Research towns. You know, to live in. It's already March. We need to decide so we can find an apartment."

"We don't need to decide *tonight*."

"We need to decide *soon*."

Kate groans. "*Love Island*, Bo. It's the season finale!"

"Zach is *not* watching *Love Island*."

"C'mon, we can fast-forward through the spicy stuff ..."

After school the following Wednesday, I take Zach to the library. Kate's at work.

While Zach pores over a brand-new middle-grade mystery series the library just got, I set myself up at a table at the far edge of the room. Back to the wall. Feet up on the chair opposite me. Laptop open.

Last week, while Kate watched the *Love Island* finale, I researched towns by myself. And I found the perfect one. Greenville. It's cute. Inexpensive. There's a new library. The high school has a pretty good cheer team.

Most important, it's far away from La Salida.

Kate, Zach, and I have a teacher development day in a few weeks. I already told Kate not to make any plans with her friends that day so we can visit it. Tour apartments. We can pretend it's a normal school day. Jack will never know the difference. It's a little early, but it will probably be our only opportunity, so we have to make the most of it. Not to mention time the tours just right so we can travel there and back within the timeline of a regular school day, or Jack'll know something's up.

I get to work. Confirming availability, layouts, and rent in various apartments. Narrowing the list. Narrowing it more. We'll only have time to see three places, maybe four.

I'm investigating a minuscule three-bedroom home on the edge of town, trying to figure out what 1.75 bathrooms means, when a hand grips my shoulder.

"What's that?"

I slam my laptop shut.

"Zach," I whisper, turning around in my chair. "Geez. You scared me."

"You're looking at houses," he says. The way he says it, you'd think I was researching how to close down the library. Or ban books.

I try to look confused.

"No, I'm not."

Zach's whole face scrunches. "You are. Why are you looking at houses?"

His voice pitches dangerously loud. On the other side of the room, the children's librarian looks up from her computer, eyes fastened on me.

I give her what I hope is a reassuring smile and pull Zach closer to me. "Shhhh. Library voice, buddy."

"Are you leaving?" he asks just as loudly. "Like Mom?"

"I'm not leaving," I say quickly. "I promise."

"Then why were you looking at that?"

I glance at my closed laptop. It's too early to tell him.

But Zach's nine-year-old jaw is set, even as his green eyes shine with tears. His whole body trembles.

In a rush, I whisper, "I'm looking at apartments for us. You, me, and Kate. After I graduate."

Zach goes completely quiet. Completely still. Behind him, I watch the librarian turn back to her computer.

"You can do that?"

Everything about this moment feels fragile as a bubble. I wish Kate were here.

"If I have money and a job, yeah."

"You're not an adult," he says. Like I'm an idiot. "You can't get an apartment."

"On my next birthday, I'll be a legal adult. So I can. That's why I've been boxing. To save money for us to get a new place to live."

Zach leans in and whispers, so quietly I almost miss the words. "We won't have to live with Jack anymore?"

"No."

"We won't get separated again?"

Gently, I push a stray curl out of his eyes, fingertips brushing the scar near his hairline.

That night in the hospital, after Zach ran away, I asked him why he did it. His eyes welled up. He said, *I just wanted to be with you.*

I squeeze his shoulder. "No. You, me, and Kate. Together. I'll take care of us."

And Zach beams. A smile so wide, so enormous, for a moment, we're at home again and Zach's laughing at one of Dad's corny jokes while Kate makes a face and says, *Dad!* Mom — upright, not crying, not empty — brushes my shoulder as she walks by, and I'm not angry, and I don't flinch. I've never heard Zach hiccup when he's stressed, and he doesn't have a scar on his forehead. I don't lie in bed at night, unable to sleep, feeling like I can't breathe.

That will be us again, I think, at the same moment that Zach starts bouncing. Like the excitement is too much for him to hold still a second longer.

Then he throws his arms around me, holding me tight. My sore muscles protest. But it doesn't matter. I'm smiling, too, as my arms go around him, my mouth drawn upwards like the tides pulled by the force of the moon.

"You promise?" he asks.

"I promise."

Zach's enthusiasm for the Plan is a magic charm I carry with me for the next two days.

Waking up at 4:30 a.m. for training? Easy. Staying awake during class? Piece of cake. Falling asleep at night? No problem. Zach's different, too. Smiling more. Sleeping in his own room. Zero nightmares.

On Friday, as I eat dinner and change for the third tournament fight, even my usual nerves feel different. Like there's a forcefield around me.

Maybe it's dumb, being so happy about this. But sometimes I forget how good it'll be when the Plan actually happens.

Apparently, I'm the only person who feels that way.

"I can't *believe* you told him," Kate says for about the hundredth time as she braids my hair. We're in the bathroom, door closed. "We agreed to wait."

"He saw me looking at houses." I keep my voice low. "He

was about to throw a fit in the middle of the library. What was I supposed to do?"

"Lie! Like a normal person." She tugs on my scalp hard enough that I whack her ankle.

"He's excited," I say. "What's the problem?"

"What if he lets something slip at school? Or to Jack?"

"I already talked to him about that, he knows not to —"

"Did you tell him he's going to have to go into foster care again while your guardianship gets approved? Was he excited about *that*?"

I flush. "He doesn't know that yet."

But Kate's not done. "He won't stop asking me how many days until we leave. His hopes are up now. What if you don't win the tournament? What are you gonna tell him then?"

She keeps pulling slightly too hard. I don't even think she realizes she's doing it.

I hold my neck as straight and stiff as steel. "I'm going to win."

I try to forget my conversation with Kate as Jack and I drive to the warehouse. As usual for March in La Salida, the weather can't make up its mind. It was sunny today, almost warm, but the temperature dropped fast once the sun went down and the fog rolled in. Goosebumps prickle my skin as Jack and I cross the parking lot to the warehouse. There are a lot of cars tonight. More than usual. We have to park about as far from the main doors as you can get, right along the edge of the island — a thin strip of gravel and dying succulents the only things keeping us from tumbling sideways into the bay.

Inside, a quick glance at the lineup tells me I'm fourth, the last of the lightweight fights. I go straight to the bathroom to change into my boxing clothes, but there's a line. It takes *forever*. Even getting across the room to the bar seems to take an eternity. It's hot. The smell of cigarettes is so strong, I can taste it. And there are people everywhere. I've never seen this big a crowd for the lightweights.

"Where's Jack?" I ask when I finally make it to the bar, where Liam sits alone, the cutman bag already strapped across his chest.

Liam points. I look and see Jack standing a little farther down the bar, talking to two men. They're middle-aged, balding and, as far as I can tell, the only people in the whole room wearing suits.

Boss the bartender passes by. "They're all here for you, you know."

It takes me a second to realize who he's talking to. "Me?"

"You impressed everyone at the last fight, Butterfly. Winning like that? With a dislocated finger?" He whistles. "Now everyone wants to see what 'the girl' can do."

Boss slides a beer down the bar and moves away to take another order. Now that he's said it, I notice the eyes on me. But not *all* of them are the usual eyes I feel here — the creepy eyes, the glaring eyes. There are curious eyes. Eyes that measure me up before handing a bundle of cash to the nearest bookie.

One guy notices me looking, gives me a thumbs-up, and mouths, *My money's on you*. Someone else says, "*She's* the Butterfly? That little thing?"

"I like 'em little," a guy replies. He smirks at me. Wraps an arm around my waist. "What do you say? I'll be a helluva lot more fun than some fight."

I shove him away. He stumbles back to his friends, cackling.

Liam's face is red. He scoots about as close to me as he can get. "Why is everyone here so gross?"

Something inside me pulls, like a too-tight string.

Maybe because of what happened last time, when midnight comes, Tyler makes a big deal of reminding us all of the rules — *no biting, kicking, spitting, tripping, excessive holding, or otherwise unsportsmanlike behavior* — and announces that tonight's prize will be the biggest yet: $6,000.

Later, when the ref calls my name, I'm expecting Jack to lead the way. Instead, he hangs back with me, letting Liam go first. As we walk, Jack wraps an arm around my shoulders and leans in, which doesn't help my nerves.

"Listen," he says quietly. "You need to do well tonight."

It's all I can do not to say, *no duh.*

"I mean. I'm gonna do my best not to lose," I say instead.

"No, no, of course you are. You're going to *win*. But I'm not talking about that alone, all right? You're good, Bo. You've trained hard. Give this one everything you've got. Really show your stuff."

That string in my chest cinches tighter. "Why?"

Jack laughs. "Don't you trust me?"

My silence makes his face pinch. As we arrive at the ring, Jack's fingers dig into my shoulder like talons. "Just do what I say."

I don't realize that Liam is watching us until I see his eyes following me as I duck under the ropes.

On the other side of the mat, my opponent, Thunder, holds incredibly still, watching me approach with unblinking eyes. I remember him warming up near me the first night of the tournament: *I'll give her more*. Everything about him sets my teeth on edge. So does the noise of the crowd all around, buzzing like mosquitoes waiting to feast.

They're here for you.

"… Go."

Thunder is shorter than me, so I have to be careful. He'll be faster, he'll try to get in close, and any hits he lands will cause more damage. He stalks me in a zigzag across the ring, fists always ready, but I stay just out of his reach. Keep my guard up. Move constantly, feinting one way and changing directions, never letting him get close enough to start a volley.

The corners of Thunder's mouth tighten. His eyes flash.

He catches me in the center. Jab-hook-jab, right in the ribs. I keep my abs tight, absorbing the blows. His neck is straight, his head exposed.

Uppercut-hook, chin and temple. He doesn't stumble, but his head falls back.

The crowd roars.

Thunder snarls at me.

At the break, Liam gives me water while Jack crouches next to me.

"That was good, but don't let him bully you," he says. His jaw is tight. "Keep it long. Feint. Go for the body."

"I'm trying —"

"Well, try harder," Jack snaps. "End it this round."

Liam's eyes dart to me. I pretend not to notice.

The next round, I try to do what Jack said. Try to stay far enough away that Thunder can't get a good volley started. Try to feint to trick him. Try to get him in the body when he'll expect me to go for his head because he's shorter.

But Thunder's learned. Scowling, he moves like his name: rolling and constant and crackling, feet always moving, fists always coming. In the first few seconds, he gets two jabs in, a hook, pushing me back. I feint left, trying to lead us back to the center of the ring, but he follows and chases me in with an uppercut, forcing me to lean back to dodge it, stepping back, back—

I hit the ropes. I'm locked in position with my arms up, trying to defend myself, but I can't maneuver around him, *whump, whump*, hit after hit, my stomach aching as I try to keep my abs tight, as the punches keep coming.

Stop him!

I throw my arms around Thunder, clinching him, keeping his arms in place to end the volley — I can get away with it for a few seconds.

But he only laughs. His breath is hot.

"You shouldn't be here," he whispers.

Quicker than a heartbeat, he extracts his right arm from my grip.

WHUMP. His knuckles in my side, close enough and hard enough that the air is shoved out of my lungs and my body tips forward. My arms drop.

THUNK. Right in the temple.

I go down.

Cheers erupt all around me. Feet stamp the floor, making my skull rattle. I try to push myself up, but my arms are jelly, my head a lead weight.

The ref starts his count. "One …"

"Get up!" Even like this, I recognize Jack's voice. "*Get up!*"

"… two …"

I promise.

Again, I try to stand. My legs buckle, knees hitting the floor hard enough to bruise. I slide onto my side, head spinning.

"… five …"

A laugh like a hyena's. That thread inside me is completely taut, no slack, fraying the edges.

I can't lose. Zach, his smile in the library — *he won't stop asking me how many days until we leave.* If I have to tell him we aren't leaving after all —

"… seven …"

That laugh again, closer now. Thunder's leaning over me, gloved hands on his knees, not guarding himself at all. Like it's already over.

He spits at my feet. "Bitch."

The thread snaps.

I kick out. His ankles fly out from under him.

"Oh!"

He hits the floor so hard, I feel it in my bones. The crowd's roaring, the noise a thunderous, meaningless mess. I dive at Thunder, fists raised. He topples me sideways, and then we're wrestling on the floor, vinyl sticky, swearing and knuckles and fists —

"Hey!"

Hands wrenching me away, yanking me to my feet. Opposite me, Thunder is being held back by some guy who I'm guessing is his trainer, bleeding from his lip, his glare sharp as a knife.

I'm gasping for air. My blood is simmering. Hot. The ref has to pin my arms back to keep me from charging again.

"Calm down," the ref says, "or I'm disqualifying you."

"What about him?! He started it!"

"*You* kicked first, that's a direct violation of the rules —"

Thunder spits again. Shouts something. I can't hear his words over the roar in my ears, the shouts of the crowd. But it's enough to see his mouth moving.

I lunge, but the ref drags me back to my corner. To Jack.

Jack half shoves me onto the stool. His eyes burn. *"What's wrong with you?"*

Some distant part of my brain registers Liam crouching next to me, cleaning me up. The rest of me is entirely focused on Jack.

"I'm sorry," I manage.

"You're *sorry*? No kicking! No unsportsmanlike behavior! And you're brawling on the floor! You're lucky you weren't disqualified on the spot! What were you *thinking*?"

Scoffing, Jack turns away, as though he can't stand to even look at me. Something warm touches my lip. Blood. What's bleeding?

Suddenly my whole face hurts. Liam's moving as fast as he can, pressing the enswell to my eyebrow, smearing CutPro on my forehead, my cheek, my temple. I can feel my heartbeat galloping in my throat.

What if you don't win and we can't leave?

Horror washes over me, cold as the CutPro.

What did I do? Why did I let him get to me? Jack's right. I'm lucky to still be here. And Thunder will be furious now. If I thought he was a tough opponent before —

I jump as Liam suddenly takes my arm. His thumb brushes my wrist, right above my glove strap. Gently, he taps the blue line of my vein once, twice.

Quietly, he says, "You can do this."

What if I can't? But Liam's gaze is unblinking and steady and certain, like it's not even a question.

My pulse slows to a sprint. My blood cools.

"Seconds out," the ref calls.

Jack and Liam duck back under the ropes, taking the stool with them. I can still feel the ghost of Liam's thumb on my wrist.

The ref looks warily between me and Thunder as he counts us in. "Go."

The crowd screams as we both swing at the same time, fists crashing into stomachs like cars colliding. I push him back, stepping away, keeping him at an arm's length and he throws, throws, throws, bloody mouth, swollen eye, bared teeth. My arms ache from defending so much. I can't keep this up forever.

I promise.

You can do this.

I feint right. Move left. Block a jab, dodge a hook. Can I hit his head again? No. He's corrected his mistake from earlier. His chin is ducked, head low. And Jack said to go for the body.

"*Ahhh!*" Thunder suddenly roars, stepping in, swinging.

"Oooh!" the crowd cries out in unison as I stumble back, nearly fall. I'm gasping for air. My ribs ache.

But I thought I saw …

I move back in. Feint left, watching his arms. His shoulders tense, and he starts to swing with his left, while his right arm, his guarding arm, drops slightly.

I don't hesitate.

Thunk, an uppercut to his chin. His arms lift reflexively, protecting him from another head shot — exactly like I planned.

I bend my knees, putting all my strength into two more jabs directly into his stomach instead.

He isn't expecting it, isn't ready. His skin buckles, my knuckles crackle —

He goes down hard, face screwed up in pain.

The ref counts. "One … two …"

Thunder tries to get up. Once, twice. He wobbles, falls again, hitting the mat.

I'm holding my breath.

"… ten."

Applause crackles through the room as the ref lifts my arm and announces my name. Grinning, I look to my corner, expecting to see my relief mirrored on Jack's face.

Instead, I see him towering there with his arms crossed. Glaring at me.

The ref lowers my arm, ushering me and Thunder — who's standing now, screaming at the ref and Tyler and me — out of the ring.

I move as slowly as possible. My stomach feels like it's full of stones.

After, it's the usual flurry. Taking off my gloves and unwrapping my hands, wiping away the worst of the blood, cracking an ice pack and holding it to my pounding head. My fight against Thunder was the last of the lightweight bouts, so now there's a break before the middleweights start, which means everyone's moving, placing more bets, collecting money, buying drinks.

The crowd parts for Jack, Liam, and me as we make our way to the Treasury. One guy claps me on the back and says, "Good job, Butterfly." I'd smile if I couldn't see the tension in Jack's shoulders, the tightness of the back of his neck. He hasn't said a word since I left the ring.

When I try to follow him into the Treasury, Jack pushes me back.

"Stay here," he snaps, slamming the door behind him.

"Is he … mad?" I can hear the frown in Liam's voice.

My face is hot. This is exactly why I didn't want to hire Liam in the first place. Why can't Jack at least *pretend* to be normal?

"He's probably upset I almost got disqualified," I say as evenly as I can. "And, I mean, he should be. I shouldn't have lost it like that. It was really stupid."

"That guy deserved it! And who cares? You won, didn't you?"

I won. Away from Jack, I can let it sink in. I'm still in this. Soon I'll have my cut of winnings — $2,400. That'll put my savings at $4,800. And I've got a one-in-four shot at winning the tournament. *The whole tournament.*

My grip tightens on the ice pack, but in my head, I'm holding the steering wheel to my car as Kate and Zach and I leave the island behind.

I grin. "Yeah. I did."

Liam smiles back and touches my wrist with his knuckle, *tap, tap*.

Suddenly, I'm very aware of how sweaty I am and how bad I must smell, and how Liam is not sweaty at all. How, even here, he smells like soap and spice.

"There you are!"

Liam and I jump apart — when did we get so close? — as Tyler appears. He's beaming like a game show host as Jack emerges, scowling, from the Treasury. Silently, Jack hands Liam a bundle of bills. Nothing to me.

The rocks in my stomach multiply. But I can feel Liam watching, so I try to keep my face as blank as the warehouse walls.

"Well done, Butterfly! What a show!" Tyler laughs. "I've never *seen* such a betting frenzy. I think we should have all our fighters brawl in the middle of the match! It'd be good for business!"

I want to warn Tyler to be careful. Jack looks like he's contemplating a dozen ways to separate Tyler's head from his body.

Maybe Tyler senses that on his own, because he throws an

arm around Liam. "Ace. Now that your work's done, how'd you like to shadow me for the rest of the night?"

Liam perks up like a puppy offered a whole handful of treats. "Really?"

"Sure! I was only a few years older than you when I started getting trained in the business of this place. Might as well start you now. You've earned it! And you can spend some time with your old man."

"Yeah. Yeah, okay." But Liam glances at me, then Jack, then me again. "But I —"

"Butterfly and I need to get going anyway," Jack interrupts. His arm snakes around my shoulders. His fingers dig in. "Early day tomorrow. And I want to get some real ice on her head."

"Of course, of course. Rest up. We'll see you next time." Tyler claps Jack on the back, shakes my hand. He grabs Liam and steers him toward the ring. "This way, Ace."

"All right," Liam says, but he's still watching me as he walks away. There's a wrinkle between his eyebrows, his face full of questions.

"See you," I say loudly, trying to sound normal. Trying not to let my voice shake.

Down the stairs, through the club, outside. Other than the massive number of cars, the lot is empty. Even with the bass from the club so close, it feels like there's no one else besides me and Jack in the whole world. Every step makes my heart race a little faster, makes my head hurt more.

We reach the car.

Instead of going to the driver's side, Jack pauses next to me.

"Before I forget ..." Jack pulls a bundle of cash from his pocket. "Here's your cut."

I flip through it. Then again, to make sure I counted right.

"This is way short," I say.

"That's what you earned tonight."

"No, it's not, I …"

But then I look at the rest of the cash in Jack's hand. It's a lot thicker than it should be.

"You *could* have earned $2,400," he says, "if you hadn't started brawling in the middle of your fight. What you *actually* earned is a thousand."

"That isn't fair. I *won*."

Jack's face is a clenched fist. "You call that a win? That was a disgrace! You're lucky you weren't disqualified!"

My palm is flat against the passenger seat window. There's a dam in my chest, holding back everything I want to scream at him.

"Sixty-forty," I say. "That's the deal. It doesn't matter how I—"

"Of course it matters!" Jack yells. "You represent me out there. Me! My training! Is that the kind of fighter you want to be known as?"

"Who cares what kind of fighter I'm known as?"

"You should! I told you to fight your best! I told you to trust me! And instead, you may have cost us everything—"

"What are you talking about?"

"Shut up!"

Seagulls burst into the sky from a hidden place in the rocks, screaming and crying. I don't move. This is a seven.

"I pay you what you earn. If you don't like it, fight better. Do you understand?" Jack prods my collarbone with his finger. The cash is still in his hand.

My cash.

The dam in my chest bursts. "Give me my money, and I'll see what I can do."

Smack.

His hand against my cheek, strong enough that my back hits the car.

"I said, do you understand?" Jack hisses.

"Hey!"

My stomach drops. Jack is frozen, hand still suspended in the air.

Slowly, I turn.

Liam, standing there on the gravel. Face pale. Mouth open. Eyes fixed right on Jack.

EIGHT

The earth itself tilts. I brace my hand against the car to stay upright.

Next to me, Jack is silent. But veins stand out on his temples. In the cold air, his breath turns to steam.

"Look," I say, "it's not what you —"

"It's not what I think? I saw him …"

Liam runs both hands over his face, drags them through his hair. I feel like I'm in a nightmare.

I move toward him. "Liam —"

He holds his hand out to me. "C'mon, Bo. Let's go."

At that, Jack finds his voice.

"This is none of your business," he hisses.

Liam takes a step closer to me. "Yeah, it is."

"Kid. I don't care whose son you are. If you're not out of here in the next five seconds —"

"Liam," I say. Doesn't he see how Jack's clenching his fists? "Go back to your dad."

But Liam shakes his head and Jack lunges forward, grabbing the front of Liam's shirt with both hands, pulling him close.

"If you tell *anyone* …"

Jack shakes him, and Liam flinches.

"Stop!" I grab Jack's arm, trying to drag him away. But he shakes me off easily.

"Get in the car," he snarls.

"Let me talk to him."

"Get. In. The. Car."

"I can fix it." I don't even know if that's true. But I have to try. If I leave now without talking to Liam, he'll go to his mom for sure. "But he won't listen if you're here."

Jack hesitates, glaring hard at Liam, who's still half turned away, shoulders up by his ears. He looks like a turtle going into its shell.

With a huff, Jack lets go. Liam stumbles backwards, nearly tripping on his own feet.

"Fine," Jack snaps. "But if you're not home in the next thirty minutes, I'm coming back. Got it?"

I nod.

For a moment, Jack looks at Liam, and Liam looks right back.

Then, silent as stone, Jack gets in the car, slams the door, and zooms out of the lot.

As soon as the sound of the engine fades, Liam steps closer. "Are you okay?"

"I'm okay." The wind picks up, stinging my raw cheek. I do my best not to wince. "Really."

The look on Liam's face tells me he doesn't believe me. He glances back at the road. "That was a good idea."

"What was a good idea?"

"Getting him away like that. I can't believe he fell for it. C'mon." He takes my wrist, starts walking, pulling me along. "My mom's on duty tonight. She's not an officer, but she can tell us who to —"

I wrench my arm away. "We're not going to the cops," I sputter.

"Why not?"

Suddenly I'm right in front of Liam, my fists pressed against his chest. "We can't tell anyone about this. Especially not the police, or your mom, or … or anyone. Okay? You have to promise me."

Liam gapes at me. "Bo. Be serious."

"I *am* serious. Jack will get in trouble."

"He should."

"*I'll* get in trouble. So will you. And your dad. You think we won't have to tell them where this happened? What we were doing?"

"We don't have to tell them about my dad. And we're minors. Jack's the one who—"

I throw up my hands. "It was a misunderstanding! We argued and things got out of hand. He didn't mean it. It's not a big thing—"

"A 'big thing'? Bo, he *hit* you. That's no joke. When we tell my mom about this, she'll call CPS on Jack so fast, he'll …"

This time, the world doesn't just tilt. It pitches completely sideways, ground and foggy sky changing places, the world upside down. I remember the social worker's car leaving me at some random house, driving away with Kate and Zach…

"Oh, crap. Bo. Bo? Here …"

When the world rights itself again, I find myself sitting on the ground, on the smooth part of one of the rocks above the bay. My knees are drawn to my chest, my hands in fists, digging into my thighs.

Liam crouches right next to me, eyes wide. "Are you okay?"

"No police," I repeat.

"Okay. No police. I'm sorry." Liam's hands are balled in the fabric of his sweatshirt, knocking against the sides of his knees. "Sorry. Just ... sorry. We don't have to do anything you don't want to do. I just ..."

My eyes sting. The ground blurs. Liam touches my shoulder, but I shake him away.

To the cluster of pebbles near my foot, I say, "No one was supposed to know. That's why I didn't want to hire you at the beginning."

A beat. Then he asks, "How long?"

I feel flayed open. I can't look at him. I brush my fingers along the rock to my right, feeling tiny pebbles, soft dirt, and coarse sand.

"The whole time."

"A lot?"

"No." The lie comes easily.

Liam doesn't say anything. I'm still not looking at his face, but I can see his double-knotted Converse, the cuffs of his jeans starting to fray.

"At first I thought Jack was just, you know. An intense guy," he says. "But when he started arguing with my dad after the last fight, and I saw the look on your face ... I remembered that black eye. After the first fight, remember? And I started wondering. I thought I was being paranoid. But tonight, when he ..."

I look out at the bay. It's too foggy to see the city. Too foggy to see anything other than the water in front of me, purple-black in the darkness.

"I have a plan," I tell Liam. "June. The day I turn eighteen, I'm buying a car, I'm starting a job, I'm getting an apartment, and I'm going to a lawyer. I'm gonna turn Jack in and apply to be Kate and Zach's legal guardian, and the moment that's approved, we're gone."

Liam eyes are wide. "Gone?"

"Moving and never coming back." I'm not telling him where. The fewer people that know the specifics, the better.

"That's what the money's for," he says. It's not a question. "That's why you need to win."

I nod.

Liam taps the knuckle of his index finger on the edge of the nearest rock. His gaze is far away. "There must be another way."

"If there was, I wouldn't be here."

"If we tell my mom about him —"

"Liam. *Liam.*" I stare at him until he looks at me. "If you tell your mom about this, your dad's going to prison. And Jack. You and I might get arrested, too. You can forget about med school. But even if we don't get in trouble, your dad will still be gone, and so will Jack, and Kate and Zach and I will go back into foster care. We don't have any other family. We'll get separated again. I can't do that to them. Zach nearly died last time, I ..." My fists are clenched. "I *can't*."

"Okay," Liam says. "Okay. So, what, I'm supposed to pretend tonight didn't happen?" The way he says it, it's like I'm asking him to shift the orbit of the moon.

"I'm not saying you can't ever tell," I say. "But you'll help me more if you wait to do it."

Liam frowns. "What do you mean?"

"I'm keeping this ... log. Every time Jack ... every time something happens, I write it down and a take a picture. When I turn eighteen, I'm going to give it to my lawyer and the police as proof of everything Jack did, proof he shouldn't take care of Kate and Zach anymore. But if I also have an eyewitness who can back up what I'm saying …"

"I don't know, Bo —"

"It's two months. Nothing else will happen before then." Mentally, I cross my fingers when I say that. "And then Jack gets what he deserves, and Kate and Zach and I get to stay together. And everyone will be so busy investigating how crappy Jack is that they won't look into the fight club at all, and we won't say anything about it, so your dad stays out of prison. Everybody wins."

Liam sits there. Looking at me, looking out at the water. In the silence, I can hear the music from the club, distant tires crunching on gravel, the faint whistle of the wind between the rocks and over the cars. Below us, the waves slosh back and forth gently, like they can't quite decide which direction to go.

Suddenly, Liam stands. "C'mon. You need to get home before that thirty-minute deadline."

Liam is a careful driver. Drives at exactly the speed limit, comes to a full stop at stop signs. Still, it feels like we've only been in the truck for a few seconds before we arrive at the gym. The curtains are drawn, the lights off. Jack's car is parked right in front.

Liam pulls over across the street, leaving the engine running. Both his hands are still on the steering wheel, even though we're stopped.

"I really don't like this," he says. "You going in there."

"I live here."

"That doesn't make me feel better."

At the same moment I grab the door handle, Liam lets go of the steering wheel. He leans over the gear shift toward me, his whole face in knots. "You promise it's only until your birthday?"

"Yes."

"And this is what you want?"

I almost can't breathe. "*Yes.*"

"And you and Kate and Zach will be okay until then? You'll be safe?"

Kate and Zach will be fine. And me … well, like I told Liam before. It's only two months.

"Absolutely," I say.

Liam exhales raggedly. "Okay. I won't tell before your birthday. I promise. But, Bo, if anything like that happens again —"

I don't really make the decision to move. One second, I'm sitting there with one hand on the passenger door. The next, I'm hugging Liam.

I can't even remember the last time I hugged anybody who wasn't Kate or Zach. This voice in the back of my head is screaming *This is weird stop stop stop,* but the rest of me is stuck on how *not* weird it actually is. How normal it feels to hold him like this, his skin still cool from sitting by the water. Normal for his arms to slide under mine and for him to squeeze, just a little.

I feel lighter.

For one insane second, Liam knowing the truth doesn't feel quite so terrible.

Jack is waiting for me in living room. None of the lights are on. I can just make out his silhouette in the dark.

"Well?" he says.

Carefully, I tell Jack that everything is fine. That I told Liam it was a misunderstanding, that it's never happened before and won't happen again.

When I'm done, Jack's on his feet, pacing the length of the living room rug.

"Good," he says.

I'm trying to decide if I dare go to bed when Jack suddenly halts right in front of me. My eyes have mostly adjusted to the darkness, and slivers of his face stand out. His sharp nose. The lines in his forehead. His stone-gray eyes. They really are just like Mom's.

"You know I only want what's best for you, Bo. For all of us. We're family. That means something to me. I'm not like your mother. I'm not going to leave when things get hard."

It takes me a second to realize he's waiting for me to speak.

"I know," I say.

"I have great things planned for you. It's too early to tell you everything, but soon you'll understand why I felt so strongly about this fight."

Jack pats my shoulder, and I flinch away, running into the doorknob with my back.

He stops. His hand hovers over the empty air. I can't make out his expression in the dark.

The next day, I spend half an hour listening to Kate tell me every detail of some drama over cheer choreography. I do my best to nod and gasp and say "No way," even though I'm barely following anything she says.

When Kate pauses long enough to comment on the bruise

on my cheek, I say it's from the fight. I don't tell her that Liam knows about Jack. I don't want her to worry.

NINE

Tuesday, April 16

10:07 p.m. Liam: Hey

10:07 p.m. Liam: How's it going?

10:08 p.m. Me: I see what you're doing lol

10:09 p.m. Me: You don't have to ask me that every day. You can just assume everything is fine. I'm good I promise

10:12 p.m. Me: And you don't have to keep sitting with me at lunch at school if you don't want to. You're not like bound to me now or something lol

10:13 p.m. Liam: Who said I didn't want to?

Early Friday morning, three weeks after my near-disqualification, Jack tells me, "We're going to have a few guests at the fight next week. To observe you."

I look up from my calf stretches. About a hundred questions fly through my mind, but they all come down to the only one I dare ask. "Why?"

But Jack just laughs again. "No spoilers! You'll see soon enough."

I have great things planned for you.

I return to my stretches, ducking my head so Jack can't see my face. This is going to keep me up at night until I know what's going on. But I don't press Jack. He's at a one right now. I don't want to do anything that would risk messing that up, especially with my plans today. Nothing can get in the way of apartment hunting.

"Can't wait," I say, and Jack grins.

"Good girl," he says, clapping me on the back. "I can always count on you."

After training, I shower and get dressed for school. Wake Zach up and help him get ready. I find Jack's iPad in his room and double-check that there are no emails from the school about there being no class today. Kate makes breakfast. Jack comes upstairs and we all eat together, pretending to listen as Jack boasts about how busy it is in the gym.

"I'm taking Zach to the library after school," I remind Jack as he stands up from the table. "And Kate has work. So we'll be back a little late. Six at the latest."

"The library!" Jack exclaims, looking at Zach. "Sure you don't want to come to the gym, little man? You're never too young to start training!"

He laughs and laughs.

The moment Jack's gone, I change. Pull my hair up into the smoothest bun I can manage. Put on a little more mascara, a coat of lipstick. Swap my jeans and T-shirt for my one and only dress — the one I usually wear to the fights — and a cardigan I borrow from Kate.

"What do you think?" I ask her, holding up my arms to show off the full effect. "Do I look like an adult looking for an apartment?"

"I guess," she says, barely looking up from tying her shoes. She's been quiet all morning. Tired, maybe. She was still texting with her friends when I fell asleep last night. "We should go if we want to make the bus."

Getting to Greenville without a car isn't the easiest thing in the world. Kate, Zach, and I bike to the bus stop. Take the 17L into Oakland. Take BART all the way out to the end of the line in Dublin. Catch another bus there, then switch buses again. It's nearly a three-hour trip. Kate didn't want to bring Zach at all. But we couldn't exactly leave him at home. Besides, I want him to see the apartments, too.

Finally, we arrive and exit the bus, pulling our bikes in tow. No one gives us a second look. With a *hissssss*, the bus pulls away.

Kate wrinkles her nose. "Why is this place called Greenville? It's so … beige."

Some tiny, logical part of my brain registers that she's right. The bay is gone, replaced with low hills covered in dead grass. The houses are boxy and brown like the hills. The smell of dirt and dust makes my nose tickle. I miss the scent of the water.

But mostly, I see the open sky. The roads stretching in every direction. When I inhale, my lungs feel like they're expanding properly for the first time in over a year.

I smile. "I think it's perfect. Right, Zach?"

He bounces. "Right!"

Kate mutters something under her breath.

"What?" I ask.

She turns away. "Nothing."

We tour a little cottage behind someone's home. An

apartment complex shaped like a U. The first floor of a duplex. If anyone can tell I'm not really an adult, they don't say anything. They seem sincere enough when they ask me what I do for work. I take tons of pictures and make notes on my phone while Zach skips from room to room, unusually bouncy, and Kate trails behind me, unusually silent.

The problem? Every place wants a hefty deposit, proof of employment, proof of income at least twice the rent, and a credit check. I do my best to keep my bland smile in place. I didn't realize they'd want proof of employment and income just to *apply*. I won't have any of that on my birthday. I can't even get a full-time job or my own bank account until I'm eighteen, let alone have worked long enough to have a paycheck or enough credit history for someone to check.

Last, we tour a second-floor apartment in a small stand-alone building with only six units. The landlord is a tiny, sixty-something white woman dressed in all purple, her dyed-black hair meticulously straightened. Her name is Karen. In the span of three minutes, she offers us mint chocolate truffles, tells Zach he's "precious," and swears at a man who catcalls me and Kate as he drives by. She's immediately one of my top five favorite people on the planet.

Inside, the three bedrooms are barely more than slivers. The laundry room is next door, which means you can hear the machines running through the paper-thin walls. Everything reeks of cats. But the bathroom's a decent size, the kitchen comes with all the appliances, and the big living room window makes the space feel larger than it is. The high school is close enough that Kate could walk home after cheer practice. The apartment costs $250 less per month than anything else we looked at today.

"This one's my favorite," Zach tells me, peering out the window in the middle bedroom.

"Me too," I say quietly.

"Well?" Karen asks us ten minutes later as we gather in the parking lot. "What do you think? Would you like to apply? I'd love to see three sweet siblings like you in here. Did you bring your paperwork with you? Proof of income, all that boring stuff?"

"Well …"

I give Kate a look until, rolling her eyes, she takes Zach's hand and gently steers him away to look at some flowers lining the parking lot.

Karen watches them go, then turns back to me, brown eyes sharp.

Suddenly I'm nervous, more nervous than I was at any of the other tours. I clear my throat.

"We love this apartment," I tell her. All the tips I read online said not to tell landlords things like that because it gives you less power in negotiations. But it feels important to say it up front. "It's perfect. But the thing is, our parents aren't around. And Kate and Zach are still in school, obviously, so it's just me, and money's a little tight, and I'm … well, my employment situation is tricky right now. So, if you can wait, I just need time to …"

I shut up. What am I saying? I'm basically advertising all the reasons *not* to let us live here. *Stupid*.

Face on fire, I stand there waiting for Karen to politely turn me away. But she just looks at me with those sharp brown eyes. I feel like I'm being x-rayed.

After a moment, she says, "You've had a hard time."

I blink. Nod, once.

"I've had a hard time, too," she adds quietly. Her eyes are far away.

I wait as long as I can, and then I say, "I have the deposit. I can get everything else, too. I just need a little more time."

Karen squeezes my shoulder.

"Let me think about it."

At lunch the following Thursday, Liam finds me at my usual table in the back corner, which seems to be a daily thing now. I don't fight it anymore, and Aaron and Danny and the rest of his friends have stopped teasing him about it every day, but it still feels weird. As if we're putting a billboard above our heads: *Illegal boxer! Illegal cutman! Right here!*

If Liam has the same worries, he doesn't show it.

"And this," he says excitedly, clicking to another page on the Mills College at Northeastern website, "is what I want to do. It's their premed-track in the Health Science major, see? Look at all these electives ..."

"You're such a nerd." I elbow him. "Are your parents excited?"

"My mom texted, like, everyone she's ever known to brag. And my dad ..." Liam beams. "He wants to get dinner to celebrate. Just the two of us."

Those five words are so joyful, it's impossible not to smile with him. "That's great, I'm —"

My phone lights up.

Incoming call: Unknown number, Greenville, California.

"Sorry. One sec." I put the phone to my ear. "Hello?"

"Bonnie?"

"Yes?"

"It's Karen, honey. From the apartment. Can you hear me? I'm calling you from my car! Isn't that amazing? I only have a few minutes, but I wanted to let you know, I can't stop thinking about you and your siblings. You three are really something."

All the air in the room seems to have evaporated.

"The current tenants aren't leaving until the end of May, so about another month," Karen continues. "When's the earliest you could move in?"

"Um ... June," I say. My ears ring with the sounds of trays on tables, lunch boxes unzipping. "June 14th." A week after my eighteenth birthday. That should give me enough time to meet with a lawyer and report Jack.

"And your employment situation — whatever it is — it will be sorted out by then?"

My fingers tighten on the phone. "Yes."

"Listen," Karen says, after a moment. "There's plenty of people who want this apartment, but I want it to go to you, if it can. So if you can come to me on June 14th with the full deposit and proof of employment, then I'll give you the apartment on a month-to-month basis. We can see about a longer lease if things go well."

I'm grinning so wide, my face feels like it's going to split open. "Are you sure?"

Karen laughs. "I'm always sure. Does that mean you agree to my terms?"

"Yes, yes, of course. Thank you. *Thank you.*"

"You're welcome, honey." Her voice is warm and soft. "You hang in there. I'll see you soon."

The second I put my phone back in my pocket, Liam goes,

"Who was that?"

"My new landlord." *Landlord*. I want to sing it.

Liam stands up straight. "You got an apartment?"

"Yeah. We looked at places on Friday, but I didn't think . . ." My face hurts from smiling.

Kate. Zach. I have to tell them!

But Kate's home with a cold for the third day in a row. Zach's going to a classmate's house to work on a science fair project (a Jack-approved outing that even Zach couldn't get out of), and the parents said they'd bring him home after. It'll be hours before I see them again. And I want to tell them together.

"We need to celebrate," I say. "I mean, I have an apartment. You're going to college. We should do *something* for that, right?" I look at Liam, who's staring at me like he doesn't know how to react, but he's having a good time anyway. "Do you want to hang out? After school?"

"Really?"

I laugh. "Yeah, really."

"You don't have — you know. Family stuff?"

I shake my head. Jack has a pair of new clients coming in this afternoon, and he'll be busy until at least six. He won't even notice I'm gone.

The bell rings, signaling the end of lunch, and Liam stands. He beams. "Then I can't wait. Where do you wanna go?"

I look through the cafeteria window at the clear April sky. I wish I had a fight right now. Feeling like this, I could do anything, beat anyone.

"Anywhere."

TEN

Liam drives us to the navy base.

I tense instinctively — why would he bring us here? — but at the intersection, instead of turning left toward the warehouse, he keeps driving straight. We pass an abandoned fire station, a crumbling little house suspended over the water on stilts, and the remains of an old pier before the buildings disappear completely and the cracked road ends, giving way to dusty, pale dirt.

In a moment, we've reached the edge of the island. Literally. There's no warning sign. Just the end of the dirt and grass and then a steep drop-off into the bay, a cliff of crumbling sand and rocks. Succulents and weeds — some half dead, all wild and tangled together — quilt the ground. Above us, the sky is the muted, soft blue of worn fabric, stitched with wispy clouds. Sharp ocean wind stings my cheeks, nips at my exposed hands. Across the bay, San Francisco gleams in the sun, sparkling like diamonds. The city's never looked so close.

"Whoa," I breathe.

"Yeah." Liam shifts gears. "Watch, it gets better."

He turns the car around so the front of it faces the road,

helps me get my bike out of the back, and we clamber into the truck bed, leaning against the back window, looking out at the bay. Waves lap against the rocks. Seagulls dive low over the water.

It's so quiet. Like Liam has brought me to the end of the world.

"I've been to the base a million times and never seen this," I whisper.

"My dad brought me here once. I must've been, like, five or six. We ate Carl's Jr. chicken stars and skipped rocks."

Liam says the words carefully, as if the story is made of the thinnest glass. It's strange picturing Tyler here with a kid version of Liam. But not any stranger than anything else in my life, I guess.

"Oh!" Liam pulls a peanut M&M's bag from his sweatshirt pocket. He looks absurdly proud of himself. "I have snacks."

I groan. I miss chocolate. "I can't have any. That was really nice, though, thank you."

Liam pours a handful into his palm.

"This won't wreck your training diet," he says, hand extended.

"I have a fight tomorrow."

"If a little candy is going to make you lose, you probably weren't going to win anyway."

I drop my mouth in mock offense. "This is peer pressure. This is what they warn you about in health class. 'Just say no.'"

Still, I only hesitate for a moment before taking a few pieces.

Liam raises his own cluster of M&M's like a toast. "To getting an apartment."

I bump my fist against his. "To being the best doctor the world's ever seen."

Liam laughs. He tells me more about Mills. I show him pictures of the apartment, tell him about Karen. In no time, we eat the whole bag of M&M's. Liam's fingers twitch every time I take more, brushing his skin. There's a swooping feeling in my stomach that feels the way the seagulls look when they dive.

"Do you have to go back soon?" Liam asks, shoving the empty wrapper in his pocket.

I check my phone — 4:17. Since Kate's sick, I'll have to make dinner, but I don't need to start that until 5:00 or 5:30. And these are prime business hours for Jack. He'll be too busy to notice I'm not home yet.

I text Kate: *Something came up. Nothing bad. Home in time to make dinner. Hope you're feeling ok!!!* Then I set my phone beside me, face down. "I've got time."

"We don't have to stay if you ... need to get home."

Instantly, Jack seems to rise between us like a wall. All I can think about is how this is the first time Liam and I have been alone since that night.

When Liam sees me now, is that what he thinks about — that night in the parking lot? Am I just some sad thing he eats lunch with out of pity?

Liam clears his throat. "Bo, I —"

"That first night at the tournament — why did you come?" I blurt. "Really?"

He looks away, but not before I see his face. Like he's bracing himself for a hit. No. Like he's already been hit, and he's trying to act like it doesn't hurt.

I wish I hadn't asked.

"Sorry. You don't have to —"

"It's okay. You might as well know." Liam sits up. Looks

out at the bay. Takes this big breath, like he's about to dive underwater. "It's so stupid. That was the day of the pep rally, and my dad called me in the middle of it, remember?"

I nod, and Liam continues. "Well, after school, I called him back. We hadn't talked in a couple of weeks. He was in a really good mood. He said he had news and he wanted me to come home right away." Liam laughs, but there's no humor in it. "I've never left school so fast."

"What'd he say?"

Liam slouches, pulling at a loose thread on his sweatshirt without looking at me.

"He and Rachel are having a baby."

His voice sounds off. Too flat.

"Who's Rachel?" I ask.

"My stepmom." Liam tugs the sleeves of his sweatshirt down so they cover his hands. But I can still see the outline of his fists through the fabric. "Rachel wasn't showing yet, so I didn't know, even though she was a couple of months along. They'd just found out the gender. 'My first son, can you believe it?' That's what Dad said. When he told me."

An unusually large wave crashes against the rocks, *shhh, shhh*. The wind picks up. The cold goes right through my sweatshirt, sinking into my skin. Tyler's words to Liam the night the tournament opened suddenly come back to me: *I already told you I misspoke.*

"You're *kidding*," I say.

Liam sits there. Shoulders hunched over knees, hands in his lap, head down.

"Asshole." I jam my hands under my armpits, so Liam can't see my clenched fists.

But Liam keeps talking like he didn't hear me. "He realized

right away what he'd said. He told me he misspoke, that he just meant his first son with *Rachel*. Rachel was there, too, she backed him up. But I could tell he didn't mean it. I don't even … I don't think I even said anything. And then, later, when I heard him leaving for work, I just … I wanted to talk to him. Not him and Rachel. He was already driving away by the time I got my shoes on. But I saw this little tube by the front door. The CutPro. It felt like a sign or something. Rachel and the girls always go to bed at, like, nine, so none of them heard me leave. Dad was already turning the corner, but I was just able to follow him. And even when I ended up here and I knew something wasn't right, I still followed him, because I couldn't just …"

Liam fidgets with his sweatshirt sleeves. He clears his throat again.

"Like I said," he mutters. "It's stupid."

"It's not stupid."

He sinks until he's lying flat on his back, staring up at the sky. From this angle, his face is all soft curves. Forehead. Cheeks. Chin. Lips.

I lie back, too, knees drawn up. There's nothing to put my head on except the corrugated metal, cold as the wind. Liam and I aren't touching. But almost.

"He gave you a nickname. He wants to show you how to run the ring. That's something, right?"

"I guess."

"But you also don't have to prove anything to him."

"I know."

"You're awesome. Even if he doesn't see it."

Liam doesn't say anything, so I grab his wrist. Well, more like the sweatshirt fabric around his wrist. With my index and middle fingers, I tap there, twice, because that's our thing. When I look at him, those soft curves on his face flush pink, glowing in the sun.

"How do you deal with it?" He closes his eyes, knocking his fist against his rib cage. "Like, it's bad enough at the warehouse. The way everyone looks at you. Talks about you. *To* you. It's like you're not even a person. And the *injuries*. But then with Jack, too — and I know you don't like when I ask you how you are, and I'm not going to tell my mom or anyone. But … I feel like I'm carrying a bag of bricks with me all the time, even when I sleep, and I'm not even …"

Part of me bristles. I didn't ask him to worry about this.

But the rest of me cries out, *Yes!* Yes, that's how it feels. Like bricks. Like a wound that never closes.

No one else has ever understood even a part of that before.

I realize I'm still holding Liam's wrist, clutching it like a lifeline. I let go, then immediately wish I hadn't.

I tell him, "I remember my plan, why I'm doing all this. That gets me through."

"What if you don't win the tournament?"

"Then we stay until I get the money some other way."

Liam rolls onto his side, facing me.

"Don't get mad at me for asking this, but couldn't *you* still leave on your birthday? Even if you don't have the money yet? Guardianship ends when you turn eighteen. You could get away from him! Get your own place, save money until you're ready to apply for guardianship, and then —"

"No," I say.

"But —"

"*No.*" It's not like the thought hasn't occurred to me. "Kate and Zach are fine now. But if I leave and they're alone with him —"

"Hang on. What do you mean, 'They're fine now'?"

Oh, crap. "Nothing. Never mind."

The wind is quiet, the seagulls, the waves. Liam's voice is barely louder than a breath.

"Why … why does he only hurt you?"

The first few months with Jack, I'd ask myself the same thing. *What did I do?* I'd look for patterns. Try to get ahead of it, try not to do anything he wouldn't like.

It was like trying to stay ahead of a hurricane that never stopped.

My fingers hurt from how tightly they're clenched. I want something to throw. I want my gloves and the bag.

But I don't have any of those things, and I'm sick of this conversation.

"Look," I burst out, "I can handle it. Because it's only me getting hurt, you know? But if I leave them there alone, I know he'll hurt *them* instead. And if I go to the police now, we get separated, then that hurts all of us, too. We … I don't think we could survive it again. I really don't. At least we know what we're getting with Jack. At least it's just me. And like I said before. It's not that often. And it's only five more weeks now. It'll all be worth it soon. I know this is all new to you, but it's not to me, and I've thought everything through. You have to trust me."

I don't realize how certain I am that Liam's going to argue with me until he doesn't. In our silence, the world around us seems to come back full volume: the birds and the waves, the distant hum of cars on the road, a chipmunk scrabbling over the rocks. The sun's at this angle where the light hits my eyes just wrong, making me squint.

Liam's so quiet. Is he mad that I won't talk about Jack anymore?

I close my eyes.

Jack ruins everything. I don't want him to ruin this, too.

Besides Kate and Zach, you are the only good thing in my life.

I'm opening my mouth, trying to find the will to say part of this, any of this, when Liam shifts again, bridging the inch of distance between us.

Our elbows touch first. Then our shoulders. Hips. The sides of our arms, calves, thighs. His pinky nudges mine.

My heartbeats trip over each other. I'm not shivering anymore.

I hold very still, waiting for him to move away again.

He doesn't. I feel like I'm standing at the edge of a cliff above a gaping chasm, too high up to see what's at the bottom.

Maybe *I* should move.

But I don't want to. Not yet.

ELEVEN

RIIIIIIING.

"Oh." Liam sounds strangely breathless. He picks up his phone. "Hello?"

A beat. He holds the phone out to me. "It's … for you?"

"What?" I take the phone. "… Hello?"

"Where are you?"

Her voice is so loud that I have to hold the phone away from my ear. "Kate?"

"Zach's freaking out! And Jack just came upstairs! I've been texting you and calling you for over an hour. I only called Liam because I thought he might know … where *are* you?"

She's congested and slightly out of breath. Zach's voice rises in the background, but I can't make out the words.

I sit up. "What time is it?"

"After six! Jack's *pissed* you're not here —"

Suddenly it's too cold and too bright and the waves are too loud. The seagulls circle like vultures.

Liam sits up, too. "What's happening?"

I ignore him. The edge of his phone case digs into my fingers. "Are you and Zach okay?"

"What part of 'Zach is freaking out' didn't you get?"

I flinch. "But Jack didn't —"

"No. We're locked in our room. Where are you?"

"I'm coming home. Stay in the room."

"Bo —"

I hang up and crawl across the truck bed.

"What's wrong?" Liam says, following me.

"I was supposed to be home an hour ago. Kate says Jack's pissed —"

I jump out of the car and Liam's right behind me, helping load the bike in the truck bed and peeling onto the road before I've even got my seatbelt on. My hands shake. It takes three tries to get the buckle in.

Why didn't it occur to me that if the sun had moved that much, I'd been out too late? Why didn't I think to check the time? Why didn't I think to turn on the stupid sound on my stupid phone?

Liam zooms through yellow lights, drives five miles over the speed limit. "How ... how bad will it be?"

"It'll be fine." But in my head, I see it. Jack's arm raising. His fist swinging.

"Bo."

"It'll be fine," I repeat.

At my instruction, Liam pulls up by the side entrance, out of sight of the gym.

"I can talk to him," Liam tells me.

"No."

"I'll tell him it's my fault." He's perched on the edge of the driver's seat, one hand on the keys. Like he's seriously considering doing something that stupid. "Maybe if I'm there, it won't be so bad."

"*No.*" I get out of the car. "And it's not going to be bad. There's nothing to worry about."

I give Liam my biggest, best, everything-is-fine-and-you-should-believe-me smile. When that doesn't work, I take his wrist. *Tap, tap.*

He closes his eyes.

"Fine." The word sounds like it's being dragged out of him with a hook. "But you have to call me if it gets bad. And I hate this. I want it on the record that I hate this."

At first, when I walk into the apartment, I think Kate must have made a mistake — that Jack doesn't know I was gone, that nothing is wrong. Everything is quiet. The living room is empty and neat, full of light as the sun begins to set.

"Decided to come home after all?"

Jack sits at the kitchen table, in my usual chair. His body is perfectly still, the kind of still that makes me think of riptides.

He asks, "Where were you?"

"The library." It's the least offensive lie I can think of.

Jack raises his eyebrows a fraction of an inch. "Without your brother?"

I do my best not to wince. "He was working on his science project. I wanted to do my homework somewhere quiet."

"This isn't quiet enough for you?"

I knot my fingers together. "I lost track of time. I'm sorry."

Jack tilts his head, frowning. I try to keep my face blank, but it feels like he must be able to smell the chocolate on me, somehow, or the sea air, or the particular leather-and-gas smell of Liam's truck.

"I trusted you, Bo," Jack says, standing up, walking slowly toward me. "I don't set a curfew. I let you and your siblings have the run of the apartment. I wake up early, every morning, to personally train you. I do everything to help you, things you don't even know about! And this is how you repay that kindness?"

"I'm sorry." I have to work hard to keep my voice steady. "It won't happen again."

Now, his voice rises. "If you're really that sorry, then tell me where you actually were, because I know it wasn't the *library*. What was it? A party? Alcohol? Drugs?" Jack's nostrils flare, like he's trying to sniff them on me. He's an arm's length away. "Was it a boy?"

"No."

"Was it the kid?"

Fingernails digging in my palms. "No."

"I'm not dumb," Jack snarls. "I see you making moon eyes at him like a stupid little girl. Your mother used to do the same thing. We're *this* close to the end of the tournament, the last thing we need is you losing focus — throwing away everything we've worked for —"

"I. Was. At. The. Library."

With a roar, Jack grabs my shoulders and pushes me back, pinning me against the wall like a dead butterfly in a box. His face twists as his arm raises, and I turn my face away —

"Tomorrow!" I yell.

Jack freezes.

"The fight," I manage. "I can't be …"

My uncle stands there for what feels like forever. One hand digging into my shoulder. The other open and raised, fingers close together, braced.

Finally, Jack lowers his arm. A moment later, he lets me go, shoving me away. I stumble, nearly hit the ground.

"Go to your room," he spits.

Light seeps out from the crack between the bottom of our bedroom door and the floor. I force myself to pause, to try to catch my breath.

I push open the door. "Sorry. Jack stopped me on my way in —"

In the middle of the floor, huddled on the rug, are Kate and Zach. Her arms are wrapped around him, body folded over his like a cocoon. He's curled in on himself, hands clamped over his ears, head between his knees.

Hic. Hic. Hic.

Zach looks up, his face red and blotchy, snot bubbling from his nose.

"Bo?" His voice is broken glass.

Then I'm on the floor, and Zach extracts himself from Kate's grasp and throws his arms around me, tight, pushing the air out of my lungs. I'm faintly aware of the sound of heavy footsteps on the stairs. Jack, heading back down to the gym.

Suddenly, I realize how cold it is in here. And that the window screen has been popped out at one corner. And that my shoebox — containing all my savings — is out of its usual hiding spot, precariously balanced on the windowsill.

"What happened?"

Silent, Kate looks away. Zach's fingers dig into my shoulders and now he's really crying, close enough that I feel his chest shudder.

"What happened?" I repeat.

Kate's voice is flat. "Jack freaked out when you didn't come home. Started yelling. Said you'd better be dying in the street somewhere to be this late. Zach heard that and thought you were *actually* dying. He was going to crawl down the fire escape and find you. The money was for the hospital."

"Zach." I grip my little brother tighter, like I'm trying to tether him to me. I see the dried blood on his skin. I see him in the hospital bed. "You can't do things like that."

"I thought … you were … *hic* … in trouble." He can barely get the words out.

I've never hated myself so much. *Why* did I go with Liam today?

"I'm so sorry, Zach. I'm here, okay? And I'm fine. I'm great, actually. Look. Look! I have proof."

Keeping one arm tightly around Zach, I reach into my pocket with the other and take out my phone. I pull up the pictures of the apartment. *Our* apartment.

"I'm gonna tell you something," I say, passing him the phone. "But you have to keep it a secret, all right?"

He nods.

"Remember the last apartment we looked at? Your favorite?" I glance briefly at Kate. "We got it."

Zach looks up. His eyes are watery, his face streaked with tears, but the hiccups have stopped. "We … got it?"

"Yeah. It's ours."

He almost smiles.

"When can we move?"

"After my birthday." I feel lighter than air. I stand, pick Zach up and swing him around as best as I can, till I lose my balance and we both fall sideways onto my bed. Zach laughs.

I sit up, slightly out of breath. I can't stop smiling. "We have an *apartment*, Kate."

Kate's still sitting on the floor, only a few inches from me and Zach. Her back is to me.

"Yeah. I heard you."

Kate is officially on my nerves.

She sits there and watches while I crawl under the bed, re-hiding the shoebox, and while I struggle to pop the window screen back in. At dinner, she "helps" me cook, aka she stands at a single spot in the kitchen chopping zucchini and yellow squash at a glacial pace while I zoom all around her, unloading the dishwasher, frying chicken, entertaining Zach, who's stuck to my side like glue. She won't look directly at me.

And after dinner, when I try to tell her about my phone call with Karen, she gets up mid-sentence and marches away. A door slams. I can tell by the *squeaaaaaak* that goes with it that she's in Zach's room. Not ours.

Zach edges closer to me. "Is Kate mad?"

"Oh, she's just not feeling well." I fiddle with the plate we set for Jack — who's still downstairs — making sure it's perfectly centered on the table. "C'mon. Let's watch TV till Jack comes back."

We put on pajamas and make ourselves comfy on the couch. I text Liam (*All good here!!*) while Zach curls up against me. In about five minutes, he's asleep.

As soon as I'm sure he's really out, I get up and go to his room. I don't bother knocking, but I do close the door behind me.

"What's your problem?" I demand.

Kate barely looks up. She's sitting on Zach's bed, a narrow twin that gets used so rarely, it's basically still new. Everything is neat, tidy. The overhead ceiling fan/light combo is on, the fan blades barely making a dent in the stiff, stale air, the light somehow too bright and not bright enough at the same time.

"Nothing," Kate says. She doesn't even have her phone. She's just sitting there, arms crossed, glaring at the wall.

"'Nothing' is making you sulk like a four-year-old?"

I haven't seen her act like this since — well, since foster care. I may have slowly frozen out all my friends, but Kate chased hers away with torches and pitchforks. Even during our family visits, she was moody like this, silently radiating an anger you felt like the burning sun. Nothing could snap her out of it until the day Zach got hit by that car, when she broke down in the hospital room, sobbing like she was letting out five weeks' worth of tears all at once.

But what could she have to be that upset about now?

I think of Zach crying on the bedroom floor, the popped window screen. I picture sick, congested Kate trying to handle that while trying to get hold of stupid me, while Jack loomed in the next room.

Guilt pricks at my stomach. I sit at the foot of the bed, facing her. She crushes her arms a little tighter to her torso. Her cheeks are splotchy. Tear streaks stain the insides of her shirtsleeves.

"I'm really, *really* sorry I was late," I say. "Like, you don't even know how much. And I'm sorry about Zach, I shouldn't have put you in that position with him, or with Jack —"

"I don't care about that." Kate speaks so hoarsely, so low, that I almost miss the words.

"Then what's wrong?"

She squirms, making the mattress creak. She lowers her arms. Crosses them. Drops them again, wrapping her hands carefully around her kneecaps.

"If this is about moving," I say, edging closer to her, "I know it's hard to leave La Salida. But we've been working for this since —"

"I know the Plan," Kate interrupts. "But, Bo … do you really *want* it?"

"Of course I do."

"Really?" Kate sits up. "You want to graduate in a month and a half and immediately move to a crappy town" — she throws her arm out in the vague direction of Greenville — "in the middle of nowhere, where it's hot and ugly and we don't know anyone, and have to go through a police investigation and deal with social workers and lawyers and family court again, and at the end of it all, you want to work some crappy job and basically have two kids at eighteen? *That's* what you want?"

I stare at her. "That's *all* I want. I'm keeping us together. I promised —"

"You know we can't, like, follow Zach around all his life, right? He's nine and he can't even sleep in his own room!"

"He's had a hard time. When we leave, it'll be diff —"

"What if you don't win the tournament? What if you can't find a job, or CPS doesn't think anything's wrong with Jack, or the courts don't give you guardianship, or you get *arrested*? Then what?"

"What's your problem?" I snap. "The Plan was your idea!"

"I was what, like, thirteen? I didn't know what I was talking about!"

"What's that supposed to mean?"

Kate runs her hands through her hair. "It means this is

crazy, Bo! We were never going to pull this off, and now you've got Zach's hopes up, too —"

"I told you, I had to —"

"And it's not gonna happen and he's going to be devastated, but you can't see that because all you ever think about is the stupid fights and your stupid plan! Just because you don't have a life doesn't mean the rest of us don't!"

"What are you *talking* about?"

"MaybeIdontwanttoleave!"

Spots of pink flare on Kate's cheeks. Her mouth is slightly open, like even she can't believe what she just said. But then she sits up straighter, lifts her chin a little, and repeats, "Maybe I don't want to leave."

I stare at her. It's Kate. My sister. Blonde hair and green eyes and a glare that could break you in half. But it's like looking at a stranger.

"That's not funny." I sound like I lost my voice.

"I'm not kidding. I don't want to leave. Okay?" She tugs at her shirtsleeves, and I think about how quiet she gets whenever I bring up any part of the Plan. How she'll change the subject. Walk away.

"I like it here. I *love* it. Our school, and cheer, and the beach and the fog, and my friends, and —"

"Jack." I spit his name. "You know all of that means living with him, right?"

"He's not so bad."

"Not so bad?"

Kate winces. "I just meant, you know, if you want to leave, I get that. Totally. But that doesn't mean Zach and I have to go, too."

I flinch as if Kate just slapped me. Leave? Without her and

Zach? There's no universe where I could ever, *would* ever do that to them.

But apparently my sister doesn't feel the same way.

As if she knows what I'm thinking, Kate says quietly, "We can't live together for the rest of our lives, Bo."

"It's not the rest of our lives! Just until Zach's done with high school —"

"That's another nine years! You're gonna do this for *nine years*?"

"Yes! That was always the plan, Kate. *We stay together*. The last time we were apart, Zach nearly died. Or did you forget?"

"He got a couple stitches on his forehead."

"He was hit by a car! And you saw him tonight. If you hadn't stopped him from crawling down the fire escape —"

For a moment, I'm lost in awful possibilities. Zach falling down the rusty ladder rungs. Zach wandering the streets alone as night falls, calling my name. Zach getting picked up by the police and brought back here to an angry Jack …

"If I'm gone," I say, "who do you think Jack's going to hurt instead?"

Kate's pink face turns red.

"I can handle Jack," she insists. "I'm doing it now, aren't I?"

There's a hot, prickling feeling building under my collarbone, spreading up my neck. *She* handles Jack? Is she kidding?

In my silence, Kate sits up and leans toward me. Her eyes fill with tears.

"I could do it, Bo. I could. And Emmy and Maya and Daniel and Alex, all my friends, I can't just —"

Thick and fast, the tears fall.

I reach for her. "Kate —"

"— and you have Liam now," she says desperately. "I've

seen him eating lunch with you, and I've seen you texting him. And you must have been having fun today because you've never been home late before. I heard he's going to Mills. That's only twenty minutes away! You don't have to leave him."

"That's not … I don't … that doesn't matter."

"Why not?"

"Because it doesn't," I spit, even as I think of his pinky against mine, him sitting next to me at lunch, the music of his laugh. I shove the thoughts down. "Nothing else matters."

Kate's jaw sets. "Why are you being so *stubborn*?"

"Why are you being so *stupid*?" Does she seriously believe this stuff? How can she pick her friends over me and Zach? We're her *family*.

I'm on my feet now. So is Kate.

"Why do you get to decide everything?" she asks. "You're not Mom."

"No, I'm not Mom," I spit. "I didn't leave. I'm *here*."

"Sometimes I wish you weren't! Do you know how insane you are? 'The Plan' this, 'the Plan' that, it's *literally* all you talk about!"

"Oh, I'm sorry I'm such a pain. I'm sorry I've only been half killing myself for the last year and a half to take care of you and Zach and —"

"You don't have to! You can stop any time!"

"I can't!" I'm practically screaming. "I can't! I'm the only thing protecting you both from Jack! And we need the money to —"

Kate's really crying now. "So take your stupid money and take Zach and leave in June! I don't care! I'll stay here. Zach won't care, he likes you better anyway —"

"That's not —"

"I don't need you to take care of me." Tears stream down Kate's cheeks, but her voice barely even shakes. "I get good grades. I can cook. I have friends, I stay out of trouble, and I don't annoy Jack all the time or say things to make him mad …"

I'm breathing raggedly. "Is that what you think I do?"

But Kate plows on. "He actually *likes* me. I'm better at that than you."

"Better at what?" I snap. "Being a doormat?"

The second the words leave my mouth, I want to take them back.

I step toward her. "Kate, I'm —"

Her face tightens, and she *shoves* me. Like we're little kids fighting over the TV remote.

"Get out."

"I didn't mean it!"

Kate shoves me again. And again. Till I'm back in the hallway, too stunned to resist.

She slams the door in my face.

TWELVE

The next day is Friday. The day of the semifinal.

I spend most of the day in a daze, trying not to think about Kate, or Liam, or Jack's hand raised above my face, or what's coming for me tonight. It's tricky avoiding Liam at school — I don't want to deal with his questions about what happened after he dropped me off — but I pull it off with one of my old "I need to study" lines. Kate doesn't say more than two words to me all day.

After school, Jack tells me I look like crap and sends me straight to bed. I don't fight it.

At 10:30 p.m., when I wake up, I find Zach reading on the floor and Kate already in bed, eyes closed.

"Kate," I whisper. "Can you braid my hair?"

Her breathing gets louder.

"I can tell you're awake."

She rolls over, burying her face in the mattress.

My eyes sting. Kate always braids my hair before a fight.

"I can do it," Zach whispers. "Kate showed me how, remember?"

I blink until the stinging stops. "Thanks, buddy. I've got it."

When Jack and I arrive at the warehouse a little after 11:30 p.m., the second floor is already packed. *Packed*. A tangle of bodies, the deafening boom of voices, everything reeking of sweat and Old Spice, Axe and smoke, old concrete and dust and salt.

I've never seen so many people here.

I'm not expecting Liam to be here yet. But after I change into my boxing clothes and rejoin Jack, I spot him near the Treasury, trailing his dad like a vaguely unhappy puppy.

When Liam sees me, he stands a little straighter. He nudges his dad, who grins like Christmas arrived eight months early and strides over to me and Jack.

"There she is. Our star!" Tyler shakes my hand like a car salesman. He's practically bouncing. "Thanks to you, we've never had such a night. The money we've made on drinks alone! We might have to turn people away at the door if you make it to the final. After this tournament, we might have to do this more often."

Tyler laughs. I try to laugh, too, but I'm the only one. Liam eyes Jack. Jack eyes Liam, his hands twitching.

I'm trying to think of an excuse to get Jack out of here when Tyler says, "Psychic, a few associates of mine are looking for you, if you'd like to talk to them before the fight ..."

Immediately, Jack's hands relax. He grins and shoves the cutman bag into Liam's arms.

"Absolutely. Wait here, Ace, Butterfly. Start warming up. I'll be right back."

Tyler and Jack disappear, leaving me and Liam alone. A big, scowling dude brushes past us, glaring. Liam edges closer to me, getting out of the way.

"Well. Didn't love that," he says, gesturing to the spot where Jack just stood.

I make a face. "You're here early. Training with your dad?"

"Yeah. We got the Treasury all set up, talked to some of the bookies ..."

"You'll be running this place in no time."

I mean it as a joke, but Liam stares out into the crowd, brows furrowed. "My dad said the same thing."

He leans his head against the wall, glancing sideways at me. "It was weird not eating lunch with you today."

"I told you. I had to study."

"I know." He pauses. "I was worried."

The way Liam's looking at me, I almost tell him about the fight with Kate.

But then I inhale and get a particularly strong whiff of cigarette smoke, and I remember where I am.

"Nothing to worry about," I say, tugging at the end of my braid. It's not as good as Kate's.

After that, time passes in dollops.

Warming up in the corner.

Eyeing Jack, who's leaning against the bar with a pair of balding, middle-aged men — the same guys I saw him talking to before the last fight. Tyler's "associates." Associates of what? Why do they need to talk to Jack?

Jack returning, wrapping my hands with surgical precision while Liam hovers.

And Tyler stepping into the ring to thunderous applause: "We've got *ten thousand dollars* on the line tonight, and a spot in the final! You can bet they're going to *fight*!"

When the first lightweight pair goes up, Jack tells me to watch. I'll be fighting one of these guys next time, if I win tonight. *When* I win. Because I have to keep the Plan on track. I have to prove Kate wrong, show her this is possible, that it's our only option.

"Smoke and the Butterfly, please! Smoke and the Butterfly!"

The air around me feels thick, charged, heavy, like the sky before a storm breaks. As always, when I walk up, a few people snicker. But tonight, far louder are the chants booming all around me: *"Butterfly! Butterfly! Butterfly!"* It feels like bricks stacking, pinning me in, sucking all the air from the room. I might pass out. Or barf. Or both.

Jack pulls me aside. He puts both hands on my shoulders, bending low to meet my gaze. Tonight, his eyes are the color of the morning fog, pale and soft. Almost soothing.

"Listen." His voice is quiet. "When you get out there, I want you to forget about all of this." He waves an arm around the room. "The only thing that matters is the guy across from you. Got it?"

I nod, and he adds, "You've trained for this."

"I know."

"You're ready."

"Am I?"

It comes out like a confession. I brace for Jack to snap at me — *what kind of talk is that?* — but he only squeezes my shoulders. For once, it doesn't hurt.

"You are." Jack leans in, almost like he's going to hug me. But at the last moment, he nudges me toward the ring instead. "Go be great."

Under the ropes, into the center of the ring where my opponent waits. Smoke. The name's pretty dramatic, but of all my opponents, this guy looks the most … normal. Ordinary haircut. All-black clothes. He keeps shaking out his arms, like he's nervous. I know I must have seen him fight before, but I don't remember him at all.

When I approach, instead of smirking or being a jerk or a creep, Smoke simply holds out his gloved hands. It takes a second for me to figure out that he's offering to touch gloves, the way the pros do.

I knock my gloves against his. Smoke nods.

"Good luck."

He sounds so sincere, I don't know what to say except, "You too."

The ref joins us in the middle. "Fighters ready?"

We both step back, getting into position. The crowd thunders and shouts, loud enough that I miss the countdown completely, except for one word.

"Go."

I bounce in place, fists up, watching, waiting. Hook, Strike, Thunder — every man I've ever fought here — they've all made the first move.

Not Smoke. Like me, he bounces in place. Head ducked. Eyes focused. Fists raised and still. His face is as smooth and blank as the bay on a windless day.

The noise builds, builds, builds, pressing on my ears. My heartbeat roars with the crowd.

I step in, swinging —

"Oh!"

Cheers and groans as Smoke lands three solid hits to my stomach and ribs. Grimacing, I raise my arm to counter, but Smoke is gone. Two feet away from where he was a second ago, straightening up.

I didn't see him duck, didn't see him move.

He's fast. Okay. Okay, that's fine. I can handle that.

I swing again. He sidesteps. And again, and again, and again, and I understand, now, why his name is Smoke. He is air itself, impossible to catch, impossible to hit. Somehow I'm on the inside while he's on the outside, controlling our movement across the ring. Usually, that's me. The ring feels smaller, my options limited. He keeps hemming me in, trying to drive me into the corner.

Don't panic.

He wants the outside? Fine. Where Smoke moves, I follow — left, right again, in a circle around the center, never easing up, edging slightly closer to him with each step.

He jabs at me. I slip beneath, countering with a hook to the ribs just as the ref calls for the first break.

"Okay," Jack says. I'm in my corner, Liam giving me water, Jack crouched next to me. His eyes are alight. "Okay. You found it at the end. Keep doing that. Work your jab. Go for the body. And make him come to you. Don't give him a chance to use his speed."

In the next round, I do my best to follow Jack's advice. I wait to move until he does, securing my place on the outside. Use my jab to put him on the defensive, going for the body as much as I can to slow him down and drive him back, against the ropes.

Smoke is sweating. For the first time all night, the placid look on his face breaks, his eyebrows drawn low, mouth hard.

I get two hits in before he clinches me, pinning my arms, and we're locked together, heads bent forward, close enough to feel his breath on my face, his sweat on my arm. I struggle for a second, then extract my left arm, swinging at the same moment he does —

Fwump.

Thunk, thunk.

Humph.

"OH!"

Whumpwhumpwhump.

THUNK — crack —

The whistle blows.

I stumble to the edge of the circle. Jack pulls me over and squeezes water from the squirt bottle into my mouth while Liam presses an ice pack to my ribs and the enswell to my jaw. I swish the water around my mouth and spit into a paper cup that Jack hands me. I glance into it. Blood. Saliva. Something tiny and white — the tip of one of my teeth.

I've seen a lot of gross things, but seeing part of my tooth there, pink with blood, messes with me. Bile rises in my throat. I cough, trying to choke it back.

Jack thumps my back and grabs the cup from me, peering inside. "Pull it together. It's not even the whole tooth."

This isn't exactly comforting. But you know what is? Looking across the ring and seeing Smoke's cutman lowkey freaking out about the swollen eye and the fat lip I gave him. His coach is right next to him, talking nonstop, hands waving wildly.

But Smoke isn't looking at him. He's looking at me. His knee bounces relentlessly.

I smile at him.

Round three, dancing around each other.

Round four, my back against the ropes, Smoke's fists in my ribs and my head, my knees hitting the mat, saved by the whistle and Liam's miraculous work as he wipes the blood from my face with one hand and holds an ice pack to my ribs with the other, leaning in close to apply more pressure, the cold numbing and stinging at the same time. He applies the CutPro, his eyes focused, eyebrows pulled low, mouth slightly open. The spotlight above his head makes his hair glow.

Round five, Smoke is sloppy and furious and wild, moving fast but throwing faster, jabs like lightning, and I am countering, trying to press him back, back, back, *whumpwhump-whump* in the ribs, the stomach, trying to slow him, trying to send him to the floor. We're both gasping for air, both drenched in sweat.

The audience is screaming. It seems impossible that the club below can't hear it.

Thunk. Smoke's jab catches me in the forehead. Instantly, I'm bleeding. A lot. I brush at my eyes, wiping some of the blood away so I can see better to counter.

I get two hits in before my eyes start to sting.

The blood — but I've gotten blood in my eyes before and it's never hurt like this. Never made my eyes water so much. By the time the ref blows the whistle for the break, I can barely see.

An almost feverishly hot hand on my arm, pulling me to the corner. Another pair of hands immediately wiping my face, putting pressure on the cut. Still, the burning doesn't stop.

"Why are her eyes red?" Liam asks.

"What?"

I close my eyes, but it doesn't dull the pain much. "They're burning."

Jack swears. I hear him snap his fingers. "Water. Water! Now. Keep pressure on that cut —"

A beat, then water poured over my right eye, then my left as I blink furiously and press my mouth shut, trying not to inhale the water.

"What's going on?" Liam asks.

"He put something on his gloves. Bastard."

"*What*? He should get disqualified for that!"

"Sure," Jack says. "Like she should have been disqualified last time? Or Strike for nearly breaking her hand?" I hear, rather than see, Jack's weight shift. "It's a desperate move, Butterfly. Means you're close. Finish the job."

The water runs out. My eyes are only fractionally better, still stinging and tearing, making it hard to see. But my body thrums with energy. My fingers twitch in my gloves. I want to crack his jaw, want to make him —

This time, when the round starts and the whistle blows, Smoke doesn't hesitate. One-two one-two one-two, aimed at my ribs. I avoid it just in time. Somehow, I manage to throw a hit of my own and he sidesteps, and it's back and forth, one of us swinging and the other ducking, no punches landing, just air and air and air.

Chanting fills the room. *"BUTTERFLY! BUTTERFLY! BUTTERFLY!"*

I swing again, and Smoke catches my wrist with his forearm and hits me with his other fist, in the head again, right in the cut. I press my lips together and grunt into my teeth, my forehead throbbing, blood falling again, Liam's careful work already ruined. Blood in my eye, new burning in my eye. Whatever Smoke put on his gloves is still there.

Through the tears, I see that his ribs are open. I jab, jab, jab, barely hitting. He grunts — his arm moves, a watery blur at the edge of my vision —

SNAP.

Pain crackling up my face. Nose caving in on itself. Bone stabbing sinuses. I cry out, blood pouring from my nostrils as the crowd groans, *"OH!"* Breathing hurts. I open my mouth, but instead of air I get more blood, salty and metallic and slimy, pooling around my teeth and under my tongue, and I'm coughing, trying to get it all out, trying to breathe.

The ref approaches, but I shake my head furiously. Across from me, Smoke's whole face stupidly, annoyingly pitying. He shrugs slightly.

I spit at him, spattering the ground with blood. In my head, I see the truck I'll buy, the bridge taking us off-island. I see Zach laughing in the living room of our apartment, and Kate with us, smiling. Understanding, now, why this is the best way, the only way ...

Smoke's guard is down. I drive in, leading with a jab, pushing him back —

Back —

Back —

Almost to the ropes —

He steps sideways, away from the ropes. Moves in. Buries his fists in my side, once, twice, three times, hard enough to force the breath from my lungs.

My legs wobble.

No —

I dig my feet into the floor, clench every muscle I have. Smoke raises his lead arm again, dropping his guarding arm, leaving an opening —

I swing. *Thumpthumpthumpthumpthump*, his temple and his chin and his jaw, jaw temple chin, temple again —

CRACK —

He sways —

THUNK.

He's face down on the mat. His eyes flutter but don't open.

I keep my fists up, just in case, even as I think, *Please* —

"One," counts the ref,

"Two,"

"Three,"

"Four,"

"Five,"

"Six,"

"Seven,"

"Eight,"

"Nine —"

"Knockout!" the ref shouts. "The winner is ... THE BUTTERFLY!"

A burst of noise like fireworks. Yelling and cheering and stamping feet. I barely hear any of it.

I won.

I'm going to the final.

I whirl around, looking for Jack, but I see Liam first. He ducks under the ropes and reaches for me with a wet rag, wiping the blood from my cheeks and mouth. But I throw my arms around his neck, and then his arms are looped under mine, holding me close. His heart thunders against my chest.

"Holy *crap*." His arms are still around me but he pulls away, eyes traveling over my face, from nose to forehead to mouth to nose again. "Are you okay?"

My nose feels like it's on fire, my head hurts, everything hurts. But I can't stop smiling. "Yeah, I'm okay."

He shakes his head, grinning, and I realize how close we are. Close enough to see the pores on his nose, and those freckles, and the tiny spot of darker brown in his right eye. To realize his mouth is a little bit open. See the slight indent in the middle of his bottom lip like a tiny fingerprint.

Every muscle in Liam's neck moves as he swallows. "Bo ..."

Then there are hands on my shoulders. Jack's hands, shaking me, pulling me back to the middle, where the ref is helping Smoke to his feet and out of the ring. I spot those two men Jack spoke to earlier at the front of the ropes, watching closely.

But I don't get a chance to think much about it, because then Jack grabs my wrist and yanks my arm up while the ref announces my victory again. Applause and cheers and roars of joy thunder all around me, filling the room.

Someone starts the chanting again, and it's quickly picked up by everyone: *"BUTTERFLY! BUTTERFLY!"*

At the edge of the circle, Liam pounds the air with his fist and claps, smiling so wide that his teeth show. I am sweaty and out of breath and bloody, and I wait for him to look away. But he doesn't.

Jack grips my hand tighter, and when I look at him, he's beaming. It's so startling that I laugh, hating myself a little bit for it, but liking it, too.

No scowling, no yelling. Just my uncle. Smiling. At me.

"You did it." He laughs, a purely joyful sound. *"You did it."*

The cheering explodes as I raise my other arm and lift my face to the ceiling, and for once, I feel how Jack always says I can be. Great.

THIRTEEN

Tyler takes one look at me and declares that my nose is absolutely broken, and the cut on my head probably needs stitches. He can't fix either of those things, which means a trip to the hospital. Tyler recommends one in San Leandro, where a friend of his is the doctor on duty in the ER tonight and won't ask questions.

But before I leave, both Tyler and Jack insist on a victory lap.

First up on my room-wide tour are Tyler's two "associates." Up close, they look just as middle-aged and balding and boring as they did from afar, though the one on the left is bouncing like a toddler who's had too much sugar, and the one on the right has these intense eyes, icy blue and sharp. Neither man tells me his name.

While Bouncy enthusiastically shakes my hand, Ice Eyes leans over the ropes and says something to Jack that I can't make out over the noise of the crowd. Whatever it is, it makes Jack clap Ice Eyes on the back, grinning.

"Psychic —" I start, but then Tyler grabs my arm and pulls me away.

"This way, Butterfly. Come meet your fans!"

All around the room, Tyler and Jack lead me, shaking hands with guys, making me shake hands with them, too. Liam follows close behind. Men congratulate me, ask me how I learned to fight like that, jokingly punch my shoulder and thank me for the cash now stashed safely in their wallets. Jack roars with laughter at all of it. Tyler directs people to the bar and to the bookies to place more bets: "If you liked the Butterfly, you should really stay to watch Lucky. He's in the middleweights. Similar profile —"

Too soon, the gauze on my forehead and jammed up my nose soak through, and the adrenaline drains from my body. My muscles ache. My head pounds. Trying to smile makes my sinuses feel like they're being stabbed with giant shards of glass.

"Midas," Liam says, watching me. The name comes out sounding like *Dad*. "Her nose is broken, and the CutPro's worn off, she should really —"

But Tyler waves his son away like a fly. "In a minute, Ace. Let the Butterfly enjoy her moment. Besides, selling your assets — that's part of the business you need to know."

Liam makes a face like he just swallowed a lemon. I elbow him, doing my best to look reassuring, even as another drop of blood trickles from my nose and the word *asset* knocks around my brain.

Finally, we reach the Treasury, and they let me stop. By then my nose hurts so bad I can't see straight, and Liam's got one hand on my arm, steadying me. It's total overkill, but I don't stop him.

"Can we go now?" I start, but then Jack hands me the biggest wad of cash I've ever seen in my life — $4,000. *Four thousand freaking dollars*. $7,400 saved. Even with the money Jack docked me last fight, I'll only be $755 short of my goal. I can make up $755 somehow. Or cut something from the budget.

This is happening.

At the look on my face, Tyler grins, exchanging a glance with Jack. "Like I said. We'll have to do this more often."

What Tyler means by that doesn't become clear until "breakfast" the next afternoon.

Jack cooks my usual post-fight recovery mega meal. I've only been up for half an hour, but I'm already dying to go back to bed. Jack and I didn't get home from the ER until well after 4:00 a.m., and when I did sleep, I slept badly, every inch of my body already sore and my nose throbbing every time I inhaled. It didn't help that Zach woke up whenever I moved, or that Kate barely had any reaction to my broken nose. When I got home, all she said was "Ouch" before she rolled over and went back to sleep.

Zach's still asleep. Kate's at work. I'm planning to eat as quickly as possible, take one of the monster pain pills the ER gave me, and go back to bed. But after Jack sets the last plate on the table, instead of going back to the gym like I expected, he sits down across from me.

It's a warm spring day. Not hot enough to make you sweat, but enough that you're uncomfortable. The afternoon light streaming through the kitchen window illuminates the photo of smiling kid Jack and smiling kid Mom, hanging on the wall above Jack's head. A stack of papers rests face down in front of him.

I put my spoon down. Oatmeal churns in my stomach.

"You did well last night, Bo. Very well. You know that, don't you? That knockout at the end — you're really something special."

Jack smiles. I've seen him smile a million times, but this one's — I don't know — different. Now Jack and Photo Kid Jack have never looked so much alike. "I'm proud of you."

"Well." I genuinely don't know what to say to that. "You told me to be great."

Jack laughs. "That I did. Keep eating, keep eating! You need your strength."

He waits until I pick up my spoon again before continuing. "Those men you met last night, right after the fight. Do you know who they are?"

"Tyler's associates?"

"They're promoters," Jack replies. "For professional boxers. Male boxers, mostly, but after your performance at the first fight — a two-round knockout! — Tyler told them they had to come see you. They went to the second fight and reached out to me right after. Said they'd be back for the next fight."

My mind replays February, March. Jack's phone call in the parking lot after the second fight. All that time he spent on the phone, all that extra training for me. Jack's words before the third tournament fight come back to me with cold clarity. *Give this one all you got. Don't you trust me?*

"Of course, that's the one where you were nearly disqualified. They weren't interested in someone 'unmanageable.'" A muscle jumps in Jack's jaw, like even the memory of that still irritates him. "But I convinced them that was an aberration. That it was a sign of your passion. They agreed to give you another chance."

The edge of the spoon handle bites my palm. "And?"

Jack leans across the table, fingers clasped. His smile stretches and grows until it seems to swallow his entire face. "And they want to sign you, Bo."

I stare at him. "What?"

Jack laughs again. The sound sets my teeth on edge. "Make you a professional boxer, make you a star! Once you're eighteen, of course. They can't sign a minor. And only if you win the tournament. Which won't be an issue, obviously."

I'm imagining this. All the painkillers they gave me at the ER last night must still be in my system. Right?

"I —"

"Don't worry. Once you're signed, you can still participate in the ring, at least initially. Tyler's all for it. Said he'll promote your pro career at the ring if you'll fight for him once or twice a month. Think of the money we'll get! And I'd still be your coach and trainer. They've got a contract for me, too." Jack jumps to his feet, pacing around the table, hands gesturing wildly. "But they — we — really think you can be something, Bo. And once you're done with school next month, you can train full-time. Imagine what you'll be able to do after a few months of nonstop training! Not to mention fighting more often in the ring. And I'm already looking into pro tournament options for you for the fall."

Abruptly, Jack stops pacing, dropping into Kate's usual seat at my right.

"Think of it." He spreads his hands as though seeing our names in lights: "Bonnie 'the Butterfly' Clark and her coach Jack Nielsen, the dynamic duo."

A bead of sweat rolls down the back of my neck. After the third fight, when he must've thought I'd ruined his chances at this sponsorship, Jack was furious enough to hurt me in the parking lot, where anyone could have seen.

What would he do to me if he knew I was planning to leave our "dynamic duo"?

Jack passes me the papers on the table, which turn out to be a contract. My contract for the promoters.

"You won't sign it until your birthday, but it's all drawn up. I wanted you to see it."

Suddenly, Jack stands and — hugs me.

I go completely stiff, too frozen to move.

"We did it, Bo," Jack says. *"We did it."*

Jack goes back to work. He leaves the contract with me. I try to read it. But the words swim on the page. Everything except my name — *BONNIE CLARK* — which I read over and over and over until my food goes cold.

Jack calls me in sick from school on Monday and Tuesday. My nose is still pretty sore, and between the splint, the two black eyes the break gave me, and my forehead stitches, I look like something out of a horror movie. A couple more days of ice and rest will help the pain and the bruising. Plus, the dentist can't see me until Tuesday morning. Even Jack agrees I can't go to school with a chipped tooth. I decide that when I do go back, I'll tell everyone that I tripped on the sidewalk and hit my face. Simple. Believable. And I don't want to draw any attention to my boxing by saying I broke my nose during a fight.

Wednesday, after training, I put a Band-Aid, then a hat, over my stitches and dab concealer on my black eyes. Back to normal.

Well. Kind of.

Anyone who didn't know Kate would think she's fine. She cooks breakfast, arranging the fried eggs and peppers into a little smiley face on Zach's plate. Makes small talk with Jack. Dares Zach to race her to the first stoplight, ignoring my protests. At a stop sign, Zach tells her some joke I can't hear. Her laugh drifts back to me, pretty as today's spring weather: the bottle-blue sky, the white-capped water, the softest breeze.

But the moment Zach walks into school, Kate's smile evaporates. She turns away from me. She's barely looked at me since our argument.

"So, are you ever gonna talk to me again, or is this the default now?" I snap.

She puts her helmet on. "Are you still planning on leaving?"

"Are you still delusional?"

Her face sours. "I have cheer after school," she says flatly, getting on her bike. "Don't wait for me."

For half a second, I consider stopping her so I can apologize. Or cry. Beg. Anything that might make her understand, or at least forgive me enough to speak to me. She still hasn't asked about my broken nose or my stitches. I haven't even told her about my winnings or Jack's plans to turn me into a pro boxer.

But.

He isn't that bad.

We can't live together forever.

Sometimes I wish you weren't here.

I shift the weight of my backpack. I can just feel the edges of the Book between my shoulders.

Why is it on me to fix things with her? Why is everything *always* on me?

***

I throw myself into training.

Contract or not, future pro boxing career or not, I still have to get through the tournament. There's only four weeks until the final. As Jack says, that means "no more screwing around." Every morning, even on the weekends, I wake up at 4:00 a.m. to train. Endless running, endless drills, endless sparring with Jack. Every evening, I do just enough homework to make sure I can pass my classes and graduate, and then Jack and I take over the kitchen, talking about what we know about my opponent for the final — Kate's favorite, Bicep Billy.

"You've fought him before, so you remember," Jack tells me. "He's big, and he's fast. Likes to go for the body. One good hit and you're on the floor, so you'll have to stay out of his way. Be faster. Be *great.*"

I don't sleep much. Or well. When I do, I dream about Muhammad Ali, and clocks ticking down to zero, and stinging bees, and cash, and Jack hovering behind me, saying *dynamic duo* over and over and over until I wake up in a cold sweat.

During the day, I work on the Plan.

My birthday is only a week after the end of the tournament, which doesn't give me much time to pull everything together. Most of the stuff on my spreadsheet, I literally couldn't do earlier, like finding a car to buy, or applying for jobs, or getting furniture. Now that I have to do it, I realize how *much* it is, especially with school and graduation prep and training. At all times, there's a clock running in the back of my head, ticking down the minutes until my birthday, reminding me how much more I have to do.

I'd planned to get Kate's help with all of this. Like, she'd kill at the Facebook Marketplace furniture game. But since we're barely speaking, I'm on my own.

At least, until Liam sees me looking at used cars during lunch one day.

"Is this for … your plan?" he whispers.

I nod without looking up. No time to talk. Only research.

"Do you need help?"

I shake my head.

"The silence tells me you *do* need help," he says.

"Find me a job that makes at least fifty thousand a year and doesn't require a college degree that I can start right after graduation." It comes out sharper than I mean it to. "That's how you can help."

Liam doesn't answer. But that night, he texts me a link to a receptionist job in Modesto. Education required: high school diploma. Pay: $26/hour. Start date: June 10, the Monday after my birthday.

After that, I show him the spreadsheet. Give him every detail of the Plan. I don't tell him about Jack's pro boxing plans, and I don't tell him that Kate doesn't want to leave. Soon enough, neither of those things will matter. Jack can't force me to box if I'm not here. And I still have plenty of time to convince Kate before my birthday.

During lunch, Liam and I work on job applications. I apply to be a police dispatcher, a classroom aid, a hearing-aid specialist, a receptionist. We talk about logistics for leaving, too. How I'll open my bank account first thing in the morning on my birthday so I can pay the deposit on the apartment. How Liam will help me move my stuff out a little bit at a time so Jack doesn't notice. How I'll wait to go to Greenville until after I talk to a lawyer and CPS or the police move on Jack so I don't tip him off and put Kate and Zach in danger. It shouldn't take long for Jack to get taken away — if not to jail, then at least away from us. Couple of days. Maybe a week, max.

There's more to talk about than we can possibly fit in a lunch period, but we do our best. It's too risky to meet outside of school. And while Jack thinks I'm working on homework, or when I'm supposed to be going to sleep, I'm really texting Liam, trading info on lawyers and cars, phone plans and renter's insurance, talking logistics — or just joking around.

Monday, May 6
12:12 a.m. Me: I can't wait to get my stitches out. And this splint. I look like a zombie who got in a fight
12:13 a.m. Liam: Half of that statement is actually true lol

But the big win comes when Liam and I find the perfect family lawyer. Alexa Hernandez. She charges a reasonable amount (for a lawyer), works out of an office in La Salida, and has good reviews online. I schedule an appointment with her for 11:00 a.m. on my birthday. When I put the meeting in the spreadsheet, I get goosebumps all over.

It's happening.

Two weeks after the semifinal, Jack is supposed to take me to the doctor after school to get my splint removed and my stitches out. But that morning, his car gets a flat tire, so he texts me that I'll have to bike there on my own.

"That's crazy," Liam says. "I can give you a ride."

I'm reluctant to let Liam drive me anywhere. But the

doctor's office is on the other side of the island, and I want to finish another job application and my final English essay before dinner.

Liam waits in the car during my appointment. When I return and get back in the passenger seat, he gestures for me to lean forward. I do. He puts his hands on either side of my head, peering at my forehead, his whole face scrunched.

"Not bad," he says. "The scar only *kind* of makes you look like you're still a zombie."

I whack his arm. "What, because you could've done better?"

"Duh. Why didn't you wait eight years for me to finish med school?"

I laugh. Liam laughs, too, which is when I notice how … *close* he is. How quiet everything beyond the car has become. I'm super aware of his fingertips cradling my head, his thumbs brushing my temples.

It's the first time we've been alone since that afternoon by the water.

Suddenly, Liam leans away. Jams the key in the ignition, clearing his throat.

"Let's. Um. Get you home."

The drive to the gym is quiet. Weird. Liam keeps messing with the radio dial, unable to settle on a station. His eyes are fixed firmly on the road.

I don't tell Liam not to drop me off in front of the gym, but I don't have to. He pulls over two blocks up, on a residential street lined with trees that bend over the road like a tunnel.

Liam turns the car off. Everything feels very quiet.

"Well," he says. "Here we are."

"Here we are."

I feel jittery, desperate to leave this car and desperate *not* to leave at the same time.

Liam clears his throat again.

"Thank you." I'm not exactly sure what makes me say it. "Not just for the ride today. For everything. I ... I don't know if I would have made it this far without you."

"Of course you would have," Liam replies. "You're ... *you.*"

At the same moment I figure out he's staring at my mouth, I realize I'm staring at his. That indent in his bottom lip should be illegal.

Liam swallows.

Something about the way the light slants makes me notice, again, the freckles beneath his eye. We're so close now, I can count them. Twelve. Scattered like stars.

I'm counting them again when Liam closes the gap. Presses his lips to mine.

They're soft like water. Taste like cinnamon gum.

His hands must still be at his sides, because he doesn't do any of the things I've seen in movies: cup my face or the back of my neck, touch my chin, run his fingers through my hair. His mouth is careful. Gentle. Hesitant. But when I lean into him, pressing my lips softly back, Liam exhales into my mouth, like he was holding his breath before and can only now let it out. A warmth rolls up my spine and spreads over my whole face.

Oh.

Liam pulls away first, pink from forehead to cheeks to chin. "Whoa."

And I lean forward and kiss him again.

FOURTEEN

Like puzzle pieces, things start falling into place.

Over the next week and a half, I get contacted for two job interviews. A pickup truck in my budget comes up for sale at a used-car lot in Berkeley. Karen texts me to say that the apartment's current tenants are leaving their couch, and would I like it? I turn in my final English essay and econ project and physics lab, freeing up more of my time. I do the math again and realize that with Karen's rent being $250 less per month than I thought, if I win the tournament, I'll only be $5 short of my goal. *Five dollars!* Jack declares my training "stellar" and only yells at me twice. I don't add anything to the Book.

Plus the weather. Every day sunny and breezy, warm bordering on hot, the air clear enough to see not only San Francisco but straight to the Golden Gate Bridge.

It feels like a sign. Like nature itself is excited for me and is celebrating early.

And then there's Liam.

"Are you sure you don't want a ride?"

I give Liam a look. It's Thursday, a week and a day before the final. We're by the bike racks — me next to my bike, Liam leaning against the wall, arms folded. School ended fifteen minutes ago, and since it's the week before finals, the place emptied out fast. Liam and I are the only people here, and all the bikes are gone, including Kate's. She texted me about some algebra study group she had right after school. I'm supposed to be at the elementary school in five minutes to pick up Zach.

Somehow, I'm still here.

"I'm sure," I say, fiddling with my bike lock, "that I don't want Jack seeing your truck anywhere near the gym."

We both agreed we needed to act, for now, like nothing has changed. Even at school. It's just too risky. Better to keep it a secret. No rides home after school. No hanging out. No holding hands in the hallway or at lunch. Definitely no kissing.

It sucks.

"I just feel bad that you have to bike home in this weather," Liam says. "Why's it so hot?"

"Climate change," I say, pocketing the bike lock. "Also, you're standing in the sun, dummy."

Liam takes one step forward, then another, so he's standing in the shade with me. It's not a big patch of shade. His arm presses against my arm. I can feel the warmth radiating from him, smell the sun on his skin. His mouth is *right there.*

Liam swallows. He glances around. "I think we're —"

I pull his face to mine.

What am I doing? I think after, as I pedal down the road, speeding toward the elementary school. Beside me, the beach sprawls, showing off in the sun — water shimmering like a jewel, the wind pushing my hair from my eyes, the air smelling like water and salt, sunscreen and sunlight.

This wind. This view. This smell. And Liam. That's what I'll miss when we leave.

Only three weeks.

Ten minutes later, Zach and I stow our bikes safely in the hall. While Zach heads upstairs, I make a point of going into the gym and saying hi to Jack, something I've done every day since his blowup.

It's busy. There's a pair in the ring, another pair waiting to go up, and most of the weight machines and bags are taken. The room echoes with the sounds of shoes squeaking, weights rattling, the *whumpwhumpwhump* of leather against the bag.

Grinning, Jack waves at me from the other side of the room, where he's instructing someone on proper stance. He's right by the window. Good thing I didn't have Liam drive me home.

I wave back before retreating upstairs.

Since tomorrow is the last day of classes, I don't have any homework, but I should be studying for my one and only final on Monday (math, kill me). Instead, I find myself spending the next hour scouring my closet (and Kate's) for something interview appropriate while Zach reads on the floor. My first job interview is on Monday, after my final.

I send a picture of my "club" dress to Liam.

Thursday, May 23
4:42 p.m. Me: Does this scream receptionist to you?
4:42 p.m. Liam: Is it the office for a funeral home?
4:43 p.m. Me: RUDE
4:44 p.m. Liam: I think my mom has a blazer I could sneak from her closet. How do you feel about plaid?

I'm trying to figure out if he's serious or not when I hear feet thundering up the stairs and the creak of the front door as it's thrown open. Barely a second later, Kate bursts into the room, phone outstretched.

"Why didn't you tell me?!" she cries, pushing her phone in front of my face.

I'm so shocked by the sight of Kate in our room, *talking* to me for the first time in nearly a month, that it takes me a full five seconds to process what she just said.

"Tell you wh — oh, *crap*."

Because on the screen is a slightly too-zoomed-in but still clear picture of me and Liam. By the bike racks. Kissing.

I collapse on my bed, dropping Kate's phone and covering my face with my hands.

"Who sent you that?" I ask. "Is it everywhere?"

"What?" Zach asks, looking up from his book. "What is it?"

"You wouldn't like it, buddy." Kate drops onto the bed next to me, beaming from ear to ear. "Emmy saw you. Don't worry, she only sent it to me. I knew it. I freaking knew it!" She shakes me. "When did this happen? Why didn't you *tell* me?!"

Because you haven't been talking to me for the last three weeks? But instead, I peer at her through a gap in my hands. "You have to tell me if it's everywhere."

"It's not. Geez. Emmy's not like that. Is Pretty Boy a good kisser?"

"Kissing!" Zach exclaims. His whole face screws up. "*Gross*."

"Don't call him that," I tell Kate. But a slow grin spreads over my face, even though I try to fight it. Beneath my hands, my cheeks feel burning hot.

"Ahhh!" Kate practically tackles me. "I knew it! Tell me *everything*."

"There's not much to tell!" But I spill anyway. Well, not about everything Liam and I have done for the Plan, or about my pro boxing offer. But I *do* tell her about parking after my doctor's appointment. About the kiss. She squeals so loud that Zach clamps his hands over his ears. I crack up, and Kate cracks up, and we're both crying-laughing. I wrap my arms around her and hold her close. She hugs me back.

I feel like I'm floating. I *missed* this.

Kate sighs and snuggles closer to me. "This is perfect. Summer's going to be the *best*. D'you think Liam could drive me and Emmy to cheer camp in July?"

I stare at the top of her head, which is all I can see of her from this angle.

"I think we're gonna be a little too busy for you to go to cheer camp, Kate."

"Why?"

"I don't know. Legal stuff? Moving?"

At that, Kate extracts herself from my arms and sits up, frowning. "We can't move *now*."

I sit up, too. "Kate. Come on."

"What?"

Out of the corner of my eye, something shifts. Zach, sitting up, his hands tightly gripped on the edges of his book, his eyes wide.

"Zach. Buddy. Do you wanna hang out in your room for a few minutes? While Kate and I talk?"

He doesn't, but I give him my AirPods and my phone, make sure the volume's up loud, and close the door.

When I go back to our room, Kate's sitting on the edge of my bed, arms crossed, eyebrows pulled low.

"Kate," I say, quickly closing our door. "I'm not staying here for Liam, or for any other reason. *We're* not staying here."

"You can't seriously still want to move *now*! Not with

everything with Liam. And Jack told me about your pro boxing offer! That's amazing! And you want to ditch all that for this ... this crazy plan?"

"Look ..." I get on the floor, lie on my side, scrabble under my bed until I extract the shoebox. She doesn't know how much more money I have, or all the progress I've made.

"See?" I open the shoebox — more than twice as full as the last time she saw it.

Kate's eyes get huge. Slowly, she runs her fingers over the bills, chewing on the inside of her cheek.

"It's over $7,000 ," I tell her, closing the lid again and replacing the tape. "Once I win the tournament, we'll have enough. And I've got two job interviews lined up, two solid jobs, and a lead on a car, and we already have the apartment —"

Two spots of color flare on Kate's otherwise pale face. "I'm not leaving."

"It's not up to you!" It takes everything I have not to scream.

Kate makes this strangled sound, halfway between a laugh and a sputter. "What are you gonna do? Kidnap me?"

"I don't have to! When I report Jack, they won't let you stay here. You can come with me or go into foster care again. Your choice. But if I were you —"

"You won't do anything if I tell Jack."

Her words are the wind getting knocked out of me as I hit the concrete floor. My nose breaking. My skin splitting open, blood in my hair, blood in my mouth.

I stare at my sister.

"You wouldn't," I say.

Kate stands a little straighter. She's still flushed, but her voice is steady as she barrels on. "I'll tell Jack you're trying to leave, and he'll stop you, and, oh, boo-hoo, you'll have to stay here and become this great pro boxer and keep dating your super amazing boyfriend—"

I step toward her. I'm still holding the shoebox, but it's dented where my fingers are clenched.

"Kate, I swear, if you tell Jack anything—"

"Tell me what?"

I turn. Slowly, as if that'll change what I see.

Jack. In the doorway. He's still in his work gear—STING BOXING GYM T-shirt, gym shorts. I didn't hear him open the door. I didn't even hear him come upstairs. How did I not hear him?

Deadly quiet, Jack asks again. "Tell me what, Bo?"

He stares me down, eyes cold and unblinking. The shoebox is squished practically flat against my stomach.

How much did he hear? Maybe I can still salvage this—

In two strides, he's across the room, grabbing my forearms tight enough to bruise, shaking me. My back rams against the dresser. Something hits the floor with a crash.

"If you don't tell me *right now*—"

"She's gonna leave!"

Immediately, Jack releases me. I stumble away from him till I'm in the corner by the door, far out of his reach. Somehow, I'm still holding the shoebox.

Those three words are just registering in my brain when Kate adds, "She's been planning to move out on her eighteenth birthday. That's what she's been saving for. Not a car."

"Kate!" I gape at her. My sister's face is pink, but otherwise, her jaw is set, her gaze fixed on Jack.

How could she?

But then I remember: *I can handle him.*

She really believes that. She's really going to try to stay here, even without me.

Every inch of my skin is cold.

"She's lying," I say. "I'm not —"

Jack ignores me.

"And leave you and your brother?" he asks Kate.

"She was going to file for guardianship. Tell the police about the fights and … other … stuff. She has proof."

A muscle leaps in Jack's neck. "And this 'super amazing boyfriend'?"

"Liam."

Jack nods. His face is strangely expressionless as he pats her on the shoulder.

"Thank you, Kate. Why don't you give me a minute to talk to your sister? Alone?"

Kate hesitates. But after a second, she leaves. I can't look at her. What has she *done*?

As soon as the door's closed, Jack sits down on my bed, back hunched. His eyes rove over the room. Kate's neatly made bed, Zach's library books sprawled across the floor, my open backpack.

The space between his shoulders is taut. One of his hands is in a fist, resting on his knee.

"Sit, Bo."

I don't trust it. But I can still feel the pressure of his hands on my arms, so I set the shoebox on top of my dresser and then perch on the edge of the mattress, as far from him as I can get.

"Do you know," Jack asks, "why you never saw me growing up? Why your mom never brought you around, even though we all lived in La Salida?"

I frown. "No."

"I didn't think so." He looks at me. "It's because she left us. Our parents, I mean. And me."

I see our empty apartment, the note on the table.

"Yeah," I say. "She does that."

Jack nods. He leans back against the wall. One hand is still in a fist, knocking absentmindedly against his knee.

"She hated being at home," he says. I've never heard his voice so quiet. "When we were kids, she'd run off to the park up the street, or a friend's, or the corner store … anywhere. She used to take me with her. But as she got older, she stopped. Told me I'd be in the way. Slow her down." He frowns, his eyes decades away. "She'd travel farther and farther, be gone longer. Once — she was fourteen, I think — she hopped on a bus and got all the way to Sacramento before someone called the police about an unaccompanied minor and they dragged her back. Dad was … not happy."

Jack's hands have gone still. One of them trembles so slightly, I can almost tell myself I'm imagining it.

My uncle shakes his head, clears his throat.

"Then," he says, sitting up, his voice gaining strength, "her senior year, she meets this idiot pretty boy — your father — and runs off with him the second she graduates. Doesn't even tell me. One day she's just *gone*, and I'm stuck there alone with —"

He drags a hand over his face.

There's a lump in my throat.

Don't feel sorry for him. But I'm seeing the little boy in the picture in the kitchen, arm around his sister. I'm picturing that boy abandoned, alone. And I'm thinking of Zach in the next room, how he clings to me whenever he feels anxious. Imagining what he might become if Kate and I left him alone with someone even remotely like Jack.

Jack turns to me. "I thought you were different than her."

"I am."

"Then why," he says, standing again, glowering down at me, "were you planning to *leave*? After everything I've done for you? The tournament, the promoters. We have a plan, Bo, we have a *future*. But you were going to wreck all that, ruin my business, *abandon* us? And for *what*?"

He isn't yelling, but a thick, awful energy radiates from him, like a storm about to break. Goosebumps prickle all the way down my arms. My gaze keeps being dragged to the side, to the Book, just peeking out the top of my open backpack. The shoebox is still behind me, on top of the dresser.

"I'm sorry —"

"You're an awful liar."

"Really?" I can't help it. "Because I fooled you for the last year."

Jack snarls. A flash of movement. I raise my arms over my head, bracing for the pain …

But it doesn't come.

I lower my arms. Jack is crouching in front of my backpack, extracting the Book from its contents. He's already holding the shoebox.

No.

"You've been staring at these since the moment I walked in here. You couldn't have been more obvious." Jack straightens, tucking the Book under his arm, towering over me. A thunderstorm brews in his eyes. "These are mine now. And anything else you had for your *plan*. I want your phone and your laptop, too. No more talking to the kid. I'll tell Tyler that he's fired. I'll be your cutman next week. And if I see or hear anything about you with him, both of you will regret it. Do you understand? I see your laptop here. Where's your phone?"

I don't move. I can replace my phone and my laptop. Even the Book isn't totally necessary — Liam can back me up.

But the *money*. We're not going anywhere without it.

"I'll give you my phone," I say, "if you give me my money."

"This isn't a negotiation." Jack's fingertips are white on the shoebox.

He glares at me. I stare back, heart hammering, gathering my courage. I only have one shot at this.

I bolt.

A year and a half of speed drills kick in. I've snatched the shoebox right out of his hands and I'm sprinting down the hallway before I hear him following me.

"Bo — "

I skid into the living room. My hand's on the front doorknob when Jack catches up, grabbing my shoulder and yanking back so hard, it feels like my arm's going to come out of its socket. I cry out but manage to hang onto the shoebox.

"Stop it!" Kate yells, appearing in the hallway. *"Stop!"*

Jack growls as he tries to snatch the box out of my arms, but I press it to my stomach, doubling over to protect it. He's still got a death grip on my right shoulder, and I can't hit him from this angle. I pull him this way, that way, trying to shake him off, but he's bigger and stronger. He wrenches me sideways, as easily as you would a rag doll.

We crash into the wall. Jack releases my arm. The picture of Mom and Jack falls, glass shattering in every direction.

"ENOUGH!" Jack roars, turning on me.

SMACK.

It's not just my cheek that hurts. It's my whole face. My skull rattles in my skin.

And then, somehow, I'm on my side on the floor. Spots swirl across my vision. My hands are empty, and there's a terrible, terrible pain in my stomach.

Jack pulls his foot back again, taking aim.

"*The final!*" I scream.

But this time he doesn't care. He kicks again. In a different spot so no bones break, so nothing important bleeds, so there are no trips to the hospital. I moan into my gritted teeth. Curl in, thighs to my chest, a shield. Something beneath me crunches, and dampness warms my side. The air smells like iron. My hands are empty, the shoebox lying only a few feet away.

"*STOP!*" Kate screams, running at him. She grabs his arm, a look on her face like she'll punch him herself if she has to.

Jack doesn't hesitate.

Smack.

Kate stumbles back, clutching the red mark on her cheek. Her eyes are wide and watery.

For a moment, Jack is still. His arm is still up and his mouth is slightly open, like even he can't believe what he just did.

Then his face hardens into the same look he always gives me. He drops his arm.

"Stay out of this," he snaps at her.

He grabs my shoulders and yanks me to my feet. Everything is blinding, white. My knees hit the floor.

"You will win the final." Jack's eyes are empty caves. "And you will sign that contract on your birthday, and you will stay *here*."

I nod. Anything to make this stop.

"Good."

Somehow, I'm on the floor again. Jack has vanished, replaced by Kate, who sits me up against the wall, lays bags of frozen corn and peas over my stomach, presses a dish towel to the cut on my side where I fell on the glass.

Tears coat her cheeks. Broken glass lies all around us.

The shoebox is gone.

"I didn't ..." Kate can barely speak. "I thought if I told him, he'd take the money and we wouldn't be able to leave. I didn't think ... I didn't know he would ..."

"*Of course he'd do this!*" I burst out. "How could you —"

And then I see the red mark on her cheek, see the scratch from Jack's nails, only a fraction of an inch from her eye.

The anger leaves me like a popped balloon.

Kate throws her arms around me, sobbing.

"I'm so stupid, I'm so sorry —"

On the other side of the apartment, the slow squeak of a door opening. A soft footstep on the floor.

I push Kate away, try to shove her to her feet. "Don't let him see ..."

But Kate isn't fast enough. In a moment, Zach's here on the floor with us, and he's hiccupping, tears welling in his eyes before any of us have said anything.

"Bo?"

I grab Zach with one hand and Kate with the other, ignoring the loss of my savings and the Book that ache like missing limbs, ignoring the throbbing pain that ripples over my stomach as I crush them to me, tight enough that my fingers go numb. My whole body shakes.

I try to smile.

"I'm okay. It's okay," I tell them. "We'll be okay."

And then I burst into tears.

FIFTEEN

Friday, May 24

8:42 a.m. 555-522-8351: Hey

8:43 a.m. 555-522-8351: Ran into Kate in the hall, she said you're home sick and your phone broke. Said you had her phone and I could text you

8:43 a.m. 555-522-8351: Everything okay?

12:07 p.m. 555-522-8351: Got your yearbook. Need anything?

2:12 p.m. 555-522-8351: Dad just called and said Jack fired me? And asked to have the fight postponed? Dad was all worked up, said he and Jack argued. He wanted to know if I knew anything. What's going on?

4:01 p.m. 555-522-8351: What happened? Are you ok? What can I do?

7:18 p.m. 555-522-8351: I'm kind of freaking out. Please just tell me you're ok

10:52 p.m. 555-522-8351: Bo?

What are we going to do?

All weekend, the question tumbles through my brain, knocking against the inside of my skull like a fist. When I'm awake, I run through options and scenarios. Brainstorm. Plan. When I'm asleep — which is a lot — I dream of my savings in Jack's hands, of Kate reaching for me and her black eye, of my room at the Andersons' house, of Zach's bleeding forehead and broken bike.

"I'll win the tournament on Friday." I whisper it to Kate late on Saturday night, in the pitch-black of our room. We're lying side by side, facing each other. She pulled her bed next to mine on Thursday so she could help me change ice packs in the night, and she hasn't moved it back.

Zach is asleep, curled up on the other side of me, finally sleeping again after a nightmare that woke him up crying. Other than going to school on Friday, neither of them have left my side all weekend.

"I'll go pro. Get back on his good side until he relaxes and start saving again. Another year, maybe."

Worry pinches at Kate's eyes, at the corners of her mouth. "Can you fight on Friday?"

I shift slightly, wincing as the cut on my side brushes the mattress just wrong. Everything aches. The thought of throwing a punch like this makes me want to sink into the mattress and disappear.

"Of course," I tell her.

"You don't have to do this for another year," Kate whispers. "You're almost eighteen. You wouldn't go into foster care anyway. If we told someone, I mean. And I have some money saved. Not much. But I think it would cover a deposit for an apartment. You could go. Apply for guardianship later. When you're ready."

"Not an option."

"But —"

"I won't leave you, Kate. You and Zach, you're all I … I can't …"

Kate loops her arm through mine and clasps my hand, squeezing.

"Okay," she says softly. "One more year."

SIXTEEN

Monday, it's back to fluorescent-lit hallways and air that smells like dry-erase markers and cheap cologne and linoleum. Back to last-minute cramming for tests, running to the printer or the library, comparing outfits for graduation and summer trips and summer jobs, and *Can you sign my yearbook?* Last week's warmth evolved into a full-on heat wave, and even now at 8:00 a.m., it's sunny and swelteringly hot — the kind of heat everyone can't stop talking about.

Kate insists on walking me to my final. Literally — her arm looped through mine, her grip almost painfully tight. Her makeup is flawless, her black eye invisible.

I don't notice Liam waiting by my math classroom until it's too late to turn around. He's tugging so hard on his backpack straps that I can see them digging into his armpits.

When he sees me, he stands up painfully straight, his whole face flushing. I can practically hear him chewing on the inside of his cheek.

Kate stops. "Oh, crap."

I try not to swear. Jack was *this* close to not letting me come to school today. I only convinced him by reminding him that if I didn't show up to my final, I wouldn't graduate, and people would ask questions. I swore I wouldn't talk to Liam. Agreed to let Jack drop me off and pick me up from school, which was fine because I can't really bike right now anyway. Even told Jack to take me to school half an hour early because I figured I could go to my locker and get to my classroom before Liam even set foot on campus.

It never occurred to me that he'd be here super early, too. Or that he'd be waiting by my classroom.

Kate asks, "What should I do?"

"Go to your locker. Act normal. Nothing's wrong. Okay?"

She leaves. I smile at Liam. "Hey."

Before I can protest, Liam scoops me up, hugging me like he hasn't seen me in a year. It's a normal hug, but even the soft pressure of that makes me suck in a breath.

Immediately, Liam lets go, looking horrified.

"Oh, God. I'm sorry."

"It's fine." It isn't. My sides ache, every muscle tense.

Liam swallows. "How … how bad is it?"

"How bad is what?"

He looks at me. There are dark circles under his eyes. "Bo."

"I was sick. People get sick."

But Liam's eyes rove across my face, over the thick layer of makeup. Linger on my shirtsleeves. Navy blue and long, all the way down to my wrists, despite the heat.

"Bo," he says again, softly.

Mrs. Springer, my math teacher, arrives to unlock the classroom. I look at Liam. Liam looks at me. I feel sicker than I did before the last fight. I don't want to tell him. Don't want to risk Jack somehow finding out.

But Liam already looks like he's about to crack. I pushed

it too far, ghosting him this weekend. It's a miracle he hasn't already spilled everything to his mom.

"Fine," I say. "But it has to be now. I have to go home right after school."

He nods. "I know where we can go."

Even though the lot isn't crowded, Liam's truck is parked in the row farthest from the buildings, facing the wire fence that marks the edge of school property. Foldable sunshades cover every window. It's more private, I guess, than anywhere in school.

I psych myself up enough to pull myself into the car. I try not to wince too much, but I must not do a very good job because Liam leans across to close the passenger door for me. His face is knotted.

"What happened?"

It's hard to think straight. My very skin feels too tight and too close. My stomach throbs.

Liam's fingers brush my wrist. *Tap, tap*. Even in this heat, his hands are soft and slightly cool, just like that first night in the ring.

If I can't trust Liam, I can't trust anybody.

"You can't freak out," I tell him.

He doesn't let go of my wrist. "I won't freak out."

I breathe in. Breathe out.

Then I pull my shirt up, bunching the fabric under my bra. Letting him see.

Even for me, the bruises are bad. Hip to belly button. Along the bottom of my ribs. Blue and purple and red. On my side, halfway between the bottom of my ribs and my hip, there's a cut about two inches long where the glass from the picture frame sliced me open when I fell.

I look up at Liam, and his face is — splintered. Like a crack in a windshield. His eyes are wet.

This was a mistake. Heart pounding, I yank my shirt down.

I reach for the door. "Forget I —"

Carefully, gently, Liam gathers me into his arms.

At first, I'm so stunned, I can't move.

Then I collapse against him, burying my face in his neck. He smells like soap and spice, like the sun. My arms tighten, fingers balled in the back of his shirt. Liam's arms squeeze, but not in a way that hurts.

His words come out muffled against my shoulder. "I'm so sorry."

Something in me unspools.

"He knows about the Plan. He took all my money," I say, and then everything tumbles out. Kate wanting to stay and our argument. My pro boxing offer. Jack knowing about me and Liam, what Jack told me about Mom, and firing Liam and threatening us both if I saw him again. Jack hitting Kate for the first time, and how upset Zach was. Jack taking my money and the Book. How Jack deleted the spreadsheet and canceled my job interviews and my appointment with Alexa Hernandez and texted Karen from my phone to say I didn't want the apartment anymore and withdrew my job applications and destroyed the pages of the Book one by one in his office shredder while he made me watch, but Kate and I are going to fix it, because we have a new plan ...

By the end, I'm slightly out of breath and slightly dizzy. Maybe from the heat. Maybe because I haven't talked this much in I don't know how long. Maybe because Liam looks like he's going to be sick.

"What new plan?" he asks.

"Win the tournament. Go pro. Get back on Jack's good side and save enough money to leave."

"So … the same plan."

"No," I say, trying not to sound defensive. "I'll be able to fight more once I'm a legal adult and not in school. And Kate's going to pitch in now. It shouldn't take more than a year."

"You can't fight like this on Friday."

"Says who?" But I move slightly wrong, and all the sore muscles in my side clench. I press my lips together so I don't groan.

Liam stares both at me and past me, eyebrows pulled low, hand on the gear shift even though the car's not running.

"Bo." His voice is so quiet. "I think you have to stop."

I throw my arms up. "I *knew* you'd freak out."

Liam runs his hands through his hair, exhaling shakily. "Just. Okay. I know you've got your siblings, and that things went bad before and separation is scary, I get it, and you've got your plan and everything, and I know it's not my decision, but *please*." His hands fall to his sides. "*Please* tell someone."

"I'm not arguing with you about this again," I say. "I'm not telling anyone. *You're* not telling anyone. Nothing's changed."

"'Nothing's changed'? He could've broken your ribs. Or given you internal bleeding. You could have *died*."

"Don't be dramatic," I reply, but I can still feel it. The hard floor against my hip, my shoulder. The toe of Jack's gym sneaker as he kicked.

"*Dramatic*?" Liam sputters.

"The ring's the same thing," I shoot back. "You've watched that all this time. What makes this worse?"

"Because it *is* worse! And Kate got hurt this time, too, and

Zach knows what happened. That's *worse*. And the ring — I shouldn't have let you talk me into going there or keeping that a secret. That *place*, it's —"

"Your dad runs it!"

"My dad's an asshole!"

I just stare at him as he barrels on. "He should be in prison! You weren't there when he was 'training' me. He sells drugs, Bo. To fund the fight club. He's got about a million bookies, all these people in debt … or the way he called you an 'asset' at the semifinal and wouldn't let you leave, even though you had a *broken nose*. And when he called me on Friday, after he and Jack argued, he said …" His face screws up. "He said you were a whiny bitch and he never should have let Jack talk him into putting you in the tournament in the first place. That he was teaching you a lesson by not postponing the fight. He's not any different than Jack. I never should have cared what he thought about me. I don't want anything to do with him."

If I had to rank everyone on the planet, my favorite to least favorite, Tyler Covey would be near the bottom of the list. But something about the way Liam's attacking him, attacking the ring, makes me bristle. Like he's attacking me, too.

"If that's how you really feel," I say, trying to keep my voice even, "why didn't you quit?"

"Because I wanted to help you! Bo, do you know how *hard* it's been? All of this?" Liam looks like he did the night he found out about Jack, like thread unraveling. "Lying to my mom for months? Sneaking out? Worrying about you *all the time*? And I did it because I care about you and I want you to be happy, and you said you were okay and I trusted you, but this …" He shakes his head. His mouth opens, then closes again. "This is —"

"Yeah, I know what it is," I snap. "I'm *living* it."

All ten of Liam's knuckles are bone-white. "Then you know it's too much."

I put my hand over his and feel his fingers tremble. Sweat drips down my temple. It's so *hot* in this car.

"I know I've asked a lot of you," I say. "I'm sorry. I am. But I promise you, it will be worth it when Kate, Zach, and I are out of there. When we're together."

But Liam shakes his head again. "You can't keep using that as an excuse."

"An *excuse*?" I let go of his hand. "In foster care, Kate became a completely different person! Zach almost *died*! And I —"

"You what?"

Lying in bed at the Andersons', staring at the ceiling. Feeling like the room was getting smaller and smaller and smaller. Feeling my chest move, but also feeling like I wasn't getting any air. Like I was dying without them.

I'm holding the glove compartment handle again, hard enough that the edge of the latch catches on my skin.

Liam watches me closely.

As calmly as I can, I tell him, "It doesn't matter. You'd still want me to leave."

"Because this is *terrible*," he says. "It's *terrible*, what you're letting him do to you."

"What I'm *letting* him do to me? Are you *kidding*?"

"That's not what I —"

"Don't you dare say that's *not what you meant* —"

The words explode from Liam's mouth. "I just don't get it, okay? I don't get why this is better than foster care, I don't get how this is good for Kate or Zach, seeing Jack hurt you, I …" He taps his knee with the heel of his hand, and I can hear him breathing. His face is red, burning, bright.

Then he looks right at me.

"I don't get why everything else matters more than what he does to *you.*"

When I was little, maybe four or five, I remember asking my mom a lot of questions. *Why is the sky blue? Why do bees have stingers? Why do caterpillars become butterflies, why don't they stay caterpillars?* She was always busy, I remember, taking care of Kate, who was a baby, or doing other grown-up things that I didn't understand. All she'd say was, *I don't know. That's just how it is.*

That's just how it is.

I open my mouth. Nothing comes out. I feel Liam's words in my aching muscles, in my sore black eye, in every single rib.

Liam wipes his eyes with the inside of his wrist.

"I can't do this anymore, Bo," he says. "I can't watch this."

Panic shoots through my veins, fast enough that the inside of the car spins. This what? The fights? His dad? Jack? What does that mean? That he's going to tell his mom? *Still*, after everything I've told him, knowing what it will mean for me, for my siblings?

Or does he just not want to be around *me* anymore?

My hands are in fists.

"Then don't," I tell him.

Liam blinks. "What?"

"You heard me. Jack already fired you. I do, too. Don't come on Friday. And stay away from me. You don't have to watch anymore."

"C'mon, Bo. That's not what I meant. I'm —"

"Do you hear me?" I snap. "I don't want your help!"

Liam's head recoils like I just hit him.

"Got it," he says.

RIIIIIIIIIIIIIIIING. The warning bell, signaling five minutes until finals begin.

I push the door open, ignoring how my muscles scream and ache as I jump out of the car and set off across the parking lot. Every step away from the truck makes the pain in my stomach worse.

My shoulders are tensed, expecting Liam to call my name, to come after me.

He doesn't.

SEVENTEEN

Friday arrives.

The heat wave lingers. Even at 5:00 a.m., the air is stifling, oppressive. Jack trains me carefully. We stay inside, all the lights off except for the one above the ring, keeping to the edges of the room as much as possible, near one of the many plug-in fans set to high. Stretches. Bags. No jump rope, no running, no weights. All week, we've been careful. Stretches only, alternating heat and ice every morning and evening. Trying to maximize my recovery in only a few days. Saving my strength for tonight.

When it's time for shadowboxing, I do my best to lose myself in it. The shuffle of my feet on the mat, the air over my fists, the rush of my blood. But my stomach aches. The cut on my side pulls and stings every time I twist even a fraction of an inch, costing me precious seconds. And I'm feeling the week without training. My gloves feel heavy, my arms stiff, my legs sore. I'm drenched in sweat and sloppy. Slow.

Liam's voice reverberates in my mind. *You can't fight like this.*

Jack watches from the shadows. Silent.

After, he walks me upstairs before the gym opens — a new

habit of his that I hate. He's sweating, too. The bags under his eyes look like they were carved there.

At the apartment door, he stops. I stand as far from him as I can. I keep my eyes on his hands.

"They say a bad dress rehearsal means you'll have a great show." Jack looks me dead in the eye. Despite the heat and sweat, my skin goes cold. "You'd better hope that's true."

Mandatory graduation rehearsal is held in the football field at noon, after finals end. The field is right by the water, but there's no breeze, no shade. We have to wear our robes, line up in alphabetical order, and listen to Vice Principal Singh give a whole speech about how proud she is of us, how far we've come, blah, blah, blah.

I try to ditch. With the final tonight, I don't even know if I'll go to graduation tomorrow. But Mr. Gable, the gov teacher who's helping supervise, catches me sneaking off and ushers me to my place in line.

Right in front of Liam.

It seems like a sick cosmic joke. Like, of course my last name is Clark and his last name is Covey.

I cross my arms, staring at the back of David Chin's head while Vice Principal Singh drones on.

"Bo," Liam whispers.

I don't move. I stare really hard at Vice Principal Singh, pretending I care about processional instructions.

"Bo."

I whirl around. Looking at him feels like taking a jab square in the stomach.

"Leave me alone," I hiss.

"I have to tell you something."

"I don't want to hear it."

He swallows. His eyes are frantic. "It's *important*. I—"

Mr. Gable reappears, smiling and shaking his head, like we're goofing off in class.

"Bo and Liam! My surprise mock-trial winners. Let's save the chatting for after rehearsal, all right?" He plants his feet and politely crosses his arms, making it clear he isn't moving.

"Sorry, Mr. Gable," I say. I turn back to the front.

David Chin scratches the back of his head, like he can feel how hard I'm glaring at it.

After dinner, Kate and Zach do the dishes while Jack goes downstairs to close up the gym and pack for tonight. I try to sleep. I can feel my heartbeat through my rib cage when I lie down. *Thu-thump*. In my ears, drowning out the sounds from the street. *Thu-thump*. In my knees, somehow, making my legs bounce.

Finally, it's time to get up and get dressed. Time to put a fresh bandage over the cut on my side, cover the visible bruises on my face and legs and arms with makeup, and take Tylenol. Time for Kate to braid my hair.

We're in our room, Kate perched on her bed, Zach watching her work, me leaning against her legs.

Her phone keeps lighting up.

"Liam's calling again," she says. "That's, like, the twentieth time this afternoon. Are you *sure* you don't want me to answer?"

"Positive."

On my way out, as always, I hug Zach. His arms feel like they're going to crack my ribs. Anxiety rolls off him in waves. He slept badly last night, waking up twice from nightmares.

Kate hugs me, too. "Just come back in one piece, okay?" she whispers. "Win or lose."

On the drive, I watch the clock.

11:27. *One good hit and you're on the floor.*

11:28. *He likes to go for the body.*

11:29. *You'll have to be faster.*

Even though Bicep Billy is almost as fast as I am. Even though I can barely lift my arms. But if I stay out of his way long enough, save my strength for one good hit ...

At 11:34, a silent Jack pulls into a spot not far from the warehouse and we head inside, through the club, up the stairs. My heartbeat gets louder with every step, and I'm drowning in the sound of it, *thu-thump, thu-thump*.

"Good luck, Butterfly," the security guard tells me as he collects Jack's phone. I barely hear it over the tsunami in my ears.

Tyler's done the place up for the final. Purple streamers hang from the ceiling, some kind of decoration I can't make out papers the walls, and music plays, the beat jarring against the bass coming up from the club below. It's inhumanly hot — I'm sweating just standing here. And the crowd at the semifinal was nothing compared to this. Wall-to-wall people. Literally, bodies pressing against bodies, packed in like something canned, the air humid and stale.

Everywhere, I hear my name in the air. "*Butterfly, Butterfly, Butterfly —*"

"There she is!"

Tyler appears, the promoters following close behind. Tyler's dressed for the occasion — a navy-blue suit, gold tie, billboard smile. He hugs me like we're old friends.

"Our little star," Tyler adds, clapping me on the back. No mention of us firing his son. No mention of me being a whiny bitch. "Do you like the decorations?" He gestures to the walls. The decorations I couldn't see before turn out to be cartoony plastic butterflies, the kind you'd find at a party supply store.

They all stand in a line — Tyler and the promoters and Jack — staring at me expectantly, grinning a little too much, eyes a little too wide.

"Excuse me," I say, taking a step back. "I have to get ready."

I take as much time as I can get away with changing into my boxing gear. Slowly, I make my way back to Jack and Tyler and the promoters. I have to stick to the edge of the room because it's too hard to fight my way through the middle, where Bicep Billy is holding court. He seems taller than I remember. More muscled. He catches my eye and raises his fist, grinning.

"See you soon, Butterfly!"

I think I'm going to faint. It's too freaking hot. It's too freaking crowded. I can see the door opening again, letting someone else in. Why are they doing that? How many more people until the floor breaks, until the walls burst?

"Bo!"

Automatically, I turn toward the door, forgetting, briefly, that no one here should know my real name, let alone yell it loud enough for me to hear over everything else.

First, I freeze. Staring.

Then I grab Liam's arm and yank him over, hard enough that he winces.

"Are you insane?"

"I told you," he says. "I have to talk to you."

"Here?" For a second I forget how mad I am at him. "If Jack sees you —"

"Just listen, okay?" Liam glances behind him, at the door, before wrapping an arm around my shoulder, pulling me close, and whispering, "The cops are coming."

Around us, people keep talking. Drinking. Betting. Laughing. Music plays. The door opens and closes again.

"What?"

"Here," he adds. "Now. With all his contacts, I don't know how my dad hasn't been tipped off already, but —"

"How do you know?"

"Because …" Liam glances at the door again. He looks sick. "Because this morning I heard my mom talking about a raid on the base at midnight, and something about a club. I tried to warn you, but —"

I grip his arm. "You didn't tell her?"

"No! Of course I didn't. Bo, if you don't get out of here *now* —"

He starts to pull me to the door, but I wrench myself out of his grasp, brain spinning. The noise of the room seems to build, pressing on my eardrums, rattling my bones.

The cops are coming. Winning the tournament, saving up the money again, having a new plan — none of that matters if I'm arrested tonight.

I turn back to Liam. "Let's —"

A hand seizes my arm. Hot breath grazes the top of my head.

"I told you," Jack growls, "not to talk to him again."

For a moment, the three of us are frozen. Jack. Liam. Me. All of us looking back and forth between each other.

Would Jack really do something here? *Now?*

Then Tyler's voice booms across the room:

"Welcome, everyone, welcome! Welcome to the night you've all been waiting for — our tournament finale!"

The room erupts. Jack turns, his grip on me loosening by a fraction.

I grab Liam's arm. "Run!"

Behind us, Jack roars loud enough that the rest of the room falls silent. *"Bonnie —!"*

I shiver, but keep sprinting. Past Tyler's confused-looking security guards, past the well-dressed clubbers who stare as Liam and I bolt by. Across the parking lot, into the hot night, gulping lungfuls of warm air.

The truck appears at the far end of a row. Liam fumbles for the keys. I dare to glance back. Someone's walking out the main doors — someone tall, someone moving fast.

Then the doors click and we're inside, the engine roaring to life, barreling away from the warehouse.

"Take Fifth. Not the main road." I'm gripping the car door. "The cops —"

"Okay, okay." Liam turns, and we shoot down a different road, thinner, not as smooth. He's breathing heavily. "Is he behind us?"

"Not yet."

But it won't be long. No way Jack just lets us leave that easy, not with the fight and the prize money and the deal with the promoters still on the line. And Liam's truck isn't exactly hard to spot.

Liam grimaces. "Maybe the cops will catch him first."

As if on cue, a police siren wails. Then another. Another, another, another, too many to count. Close.

Liam swears.

"Pull over," I say.

"What?"

"Just pull over!"

He does.

"Turn the car off."

He does that, too, and I grab his shoulder and pull both of us down, so we're not immediately visible from the road. I can hear both of us breathing.

"What are you doing?" he whispers.

"In case they're on this road. They won't see us leaving the base."

The sirens pitch louder, higher. I close my eyes. Blue and red lights flash on the inside of my eyelids, car after car after car.

I've never held so still.

The lights vanish. The sirens grow quieter but not silent. The warehouse isn't far. I think of what must be half the La Salida Police Department pulling into the parking lot, storming the stairs, filling the second floor.

A pang goes through me, surprisingly sharp.

I look at Liam. Honey eyes and messy hair, twelve freckles, that dent in his bottom lip. Still here, even after our terrible argument on Monday, after countless chances to walk away.

Not talking to him this week feels like the biggest, stupidest waste of time ever.

I squeeze his elbow, the only part of him I can reach. "I'm sorry I was so —"

"No, I'm sorry. I shouldn't have tried to tell you what to do."

More sirens. We both fall silent. A new wave of blue and red lights flickers over the ceiling.

After no new cop cars pass us for a while, Liam starts the

truck again and pulls back onto the road. His knuckles are white on the steering wheel. I'm twisted around in my seat, staring at the miraculously empty road behind us, watching. Waiting.

"We have to get to the gym." I keep my eyes on the road so my voice doesn't shake. "If Jack got past the police like we did, that's where he'll go. And he's gonna be *pissed.*" I picture Kate's black eye, and my stomach rolls. "If he gets to Kate and Zach first ..."

Liam slams on the gas, shooting across the intersection. It's the fastest I've ever seen him drive.

"I'll take you all to my house," he says. "My mom will know what to do."

I close my eyes.

When we arrive at the gym, all is quiet. The blinds are closed, the lights off. The sidewalks are empty.

We circle the block a couple of times, but no police cars wait for us, and Jack's car is nowhere in sight. Away from the water, the air feels warmer. Thicker.

Liam parks around the corner. He wants to come in with me, but I tell him to wait here and keep the engine running.

"Don't worry," I tell him, hopping out of the truck. "I'll be right back. Five minutes, max."

I take off. Down the sidewalk to the apartment entrance, past our bikes in the hall, up the little staircase. I don't bother locking any doors behind me. They'll only slow us down when we leave. Everything is dark and quiet.

At the top of the stairs, I throw the front door open. "Kate! Zach! We gotta go, we —"

I look up and freeze.

Jack.

Sitting in the middle of the couch. His face is stone, his eyes jagged.

Kate and Zach sit on either side of him. Jack's got an arm around each of them, his fingertips white where they press into their arms. Zach's trembling, hiccuping with every breath. Kate sits pin straight, a blazing red cut on her cheek, just beneath her black eye. At all three of their feet rests a bag. Kate's and Zach's school backpacks, and a small duffel Jack sometimes uses to carry gym equipment. All three bags look full. Kate and Zach have shoes on, even though they're both in their pajamas.

"I knew," Jack says, deadly calm, "that you wouldn't leave without them."

Kate's eyes meet mine, then move clearly downward to her hands, balanced on her knees. Her fingers splay wide, deliberate — all ten of them.

Every inch of my body is cold. "Your car —"

"Do you think I'm stupid enough to park anywhere near this place?" Jack says, still in that too-calm voice. "I left out the other side of the parking lot. Barely got out before the cops showed up. Thanks to you and that *stupid* kid."

"We didn't —"

"Don't lie to me!"

Kate winces. Tears pool in Zach's eyes, and he hiccups again, the loudest one yet.

I shut up.

Jack inhales deeply. His eyes close, then open again.

"Go to your room," he tells me. "Pack your things. Necessities only. You have three minutes."

Our room is a mess. Every dresser drawer is open, clothes spilling out. Zach's library books and shoes are strewn all over the floor, the contents of Kate's and Zach's backpacks dumped on Kate's bed. Kate's phone and laptop are smashed.

I try not to picture what might've happened to make the room look this way, to put that mark on Kate's face.

When I return to the living room, Jack, Kate, and Zach are all standing. Kate and Zach have their backpacks on. Jack's duffel is slung over his back. Jack's still holding each of them by the arms.

"Open the door," he says.

I do.

"Go downstairs."

I start walking because my heart's pounding so loud I can't think, because I don't want an angry Jack anywhere near the top of a staircase while he's still holding my siblings like that.

"Where are we going?" Kate asks.

"Somewhere the police can't find us," Jack says. "Somewhere your sister can't *run*."

Through the door at the bottom of the stairs and into the hallway. I turn right, toward the door leading to the street.

But Jack says, "No. Through the gym."

The gym is dark, lit only by the faint orange glow of the streetlight through the closed blinds. I move as slowly as I think I can get away with, listening to the shuffle of three pairs of feet on the floor behind me and Zach sniffling.

The night Jack took my money, I barely lasted more than a minute against him. I don't think I can get both Kate and Zach away from Jack here, not without putting them in even more danger. But if we're going to the car, he'll have to let go of Kate and Zach at some —

Thunk.

I whirl around just in time to see the door at the back of

the gym swing closed again. To see the silhouette of a tall, messy-haired figure sprint across the room to us and punch Jack right in the face.

It's an awful hit. Bad form. Thumb inside his fist. Not much power. But it's enough to make Jack release Kate and Zach and clutch his face. Kate grabs Zach and they both stumble back, away from Jack, reaching for me. I crush them to me while glaring at the figure on the other side of Jack, his features slowly becoming clear in the dark.

Liam cradles his hand to his chest, face twisted in pain.

"I told you to stay in the truck!"

Ignoring me, Liam grabs my arm with his good hand and starts pulling us toward the front door. "C'mon!"

We run. Zach's hand in mine, Kate on his other side, Liam on my left. I touch the doorknob—

Liam disappears from my peripheral vision.

THUD.

I push Zach and Kate behind me before I turn. Liam, on the floor by Jack's office. Jack, towering above him, kicking—

SNAP.

Liam cries out, his hands flying up to cover his nose. Something black drips between his fingers, pooling on the floor.

"This is your fault!" Jack screams at him.

Still curled up in pain, Liam glances up and tosses something to me. They hit the floor. His car keys.

"Go!"

I grab the keys. Shove them into Kate's hands and push her toward the door. "He parked around the corner. Take Zach and go. Call the police."

Her face is white. "I'm not leaving you!"

But I'm already throwing off my backpack and running as

Jack kicks again. Liam twitches in this way that makes me think of someone getting shocked back to life in a hospital on TV.

Rage floods my body, white-hot.

I ram into Jack shoulder-first. When he crashes to the ground, his head hits the baseboard. He groans, rolling face down onto the floor. I reach for Liam, throwing his arm over my shoulder. When I try to lift him, I almost fall, too. He's taller than me and dead weight. I slip back to the floor beside him.

"Liam." I shake his shoulder. A cut on his temple, lip split open, nose definitely broken. Blood all over his face, the front of his shirt. His chest moves shallowly, too quick. "*Liam*. Get up, you have to get up."

Behind me, Jack groans again.

Liam doesn't move. I shake him again. I can't leave him here, not with Jack like this.

"Liam. *Liam* —"

"AHHHH!"

I jump at the sudden roar, and there are hands on my arms, tight enough that I gasp, dragging me back —

And the hands are gone.

Instantly I'm on my feet, fists raised. But I'm already too late. Jack throws Kate off him. She must have pulled him away from me.

Thunk. She crashes into the nearest punching bag. Crumples to the floor, the bag swinging, chain rattling.

I blink and I'm kneeling next to her, crushing her hand in mine, shaking her.

"Kate. *Kate!*" But she's like Liam. Her eyes are closed. When I touch the back of her head, my fingertips come away wet, and she groans. Her eyelids flutter.

Suddenly, a voice behind me.

"My sister is in trouble."

I spin. Zach is standing by the door where I left him. Somehow, impossibly, he's holding my phone to his ear. Talking.

Two yards away, Jack stands. Frozen. His mouth is open.

"My uncle's hurting her and he ... *hic* ... hurt my other sister, too," Zach says. Every inch of him shakes, but he doesn't let go of the phone. "We're at ...*hic*... Sting Boxing Gym in La Salida, we need —"

The phone crashes to the ground as Jack grabs my little brother.

"Do you know what you just did?"

I run.

But Jack's legs are longer, and he's faster. He drags Zach back across the floor till he crashes into the steps leading up to the ring.

By the time I catch up, Jack is already standing on the other side of the ring, at the very edge, lifting Zach by his neck and dangling him over the ropes. Zach's feet flail wildly, his face turning red, then purple.

I am frozen, my feet bolted to the mat.

This isn't real.

But I can hear Zach whimpering.

"Let him go." I feel my mouth move, but my voice sounds far away.

A vein pulses in my uncle's neck. His eyes are a wildfire.

"Only," Jack says, in that deadly calm voice, "if you promise me that once I do, we will leave this place, and you won't try to run, ever again."

He raises Zach higher, and Zach makes this awful sound as he tries to breathe, gasping and wet.

"I promise!" I yell. "Let him go!"

Slowly, Jack's head tilts. "Fine."

Jack drops him.

THUD.

CRACK.

Zach screams. I run for the steps, but Jack intercepts me, dragging me away from the edge to the center of the ring.

I can hear my little brother crying somewhere on the floor, out of sight.

I wrestle myself out of Jack's grip and turn to face him, my fists raised, jaw clenched, blood screaming —

Crack. Thwump. Thwump. Oomph. Knuckles digging into flesh, bone against bone, hot breath on my face, my knuckles in his head, his fists in my side. Blood on my hands, blood on Jack's hands, blood on the floor.

I hit the ropes. My back is to the rest of the room, and all I can see is Jack.

"Zach!" I call, not knowing how badly he's hurt, not knowing what's going on, praying he can't see what's happening to me. "Get Kate and —"

But Jack moves in. I try to hit him, but he's his nickname. The Psychic blocks every move I make faster than I can think. He grabs my arm and pins it to my side. His other hand crashes into my unprotected ribs, once, twice, three times, four —

Crack.

I scream. That makes the pain worse. A broken rib, at least.

Jack's cackling. His teeth flash. "Fists up, Butterfly! Fists up!"

The words flip a switch in me. Everything Jack's ever said to me seems to flood my brain, pressing on some invisible dam. *Fists up, you could be great, family sticks together, I'm not asking, what's wrong with you, I can always count on you, you'll both regret it, you will stay here —*

I forget stance and technique and everything Jack's ever taught me, and dive —

Jack's on the floor and I'm kneeling above him, *whump, whump, whump*. He tries to block, but I am done floating. I sting and sting and sting. Flesh buckling, bone crackling, Jack crying out, and a whisper, *"Bonnie —"*

At some point, I realize Jack isn't moving anymore.

I stand up, out of his reach, and watch. My chest heaves. I'm drenched in sweat.

Jack's eyes are closed.

The Butterfly wins, I think, dizzy. I picture the ref at my side. He raises my arm. The crowd roars.

Then, in the distance, a siren wails.

Somehow my knees are on the ground, beside Jack again. He's sprawled, feet pointed out, arms spread wide. Eyes still closed. His face is swollen and torn. A gash on his forehead bleeds freely down his scalp, pooling on the ring beneath him.

I did this.

Blue and red lights suddenly fill the room, striping the walls, illuminating Jack's beaten-up face and my torn, bloody hands.

The front door crashes open.

I give in. I close my eyes.

EIGHTEEN

"Do you know where you are, Bonnie?"

"What's your pain on a scale of one to ten?"

Doctors and nurses circling. Blinking. Thoughts moving like syrup. Aching everywhere. Squinting at the strip lights above me.

Finally, I'm awake enough to fumble for the bed remote and sit up, despite the pain in my ribs and the nurse's fussing.

"Where are my —"

They're right here.

Liam. In a blue hospital gown like mine, pulling an IV. Stitches in his eyebrow and in his lip. Swelling and bruising all over his face. A splint across his nose and a cast on his thumb.

Kate. A black eye. Stitches on the cut on her cheek. Bruises and scrapes on her arms. A thick white bandage tied around her head. Bags under her eyes like she hasn't slept in days. When I look at her, her shoulders sag, like she's just been relieved of some huge invisible weight.

And Zach. More bruises than skin, his wrist in a thick cast.

"How do you feel?" Kate asks.

I use the remote on the bed to sit up more, as much as I

can bear. Then I crush all of them to me, ignoring the awful twinge in my ribs and the nurse's protests: "Be *careful*!"

I only squeeze the three of them tighter. I don't think I could possibly hold them close enough.

They're okay.

I clutch my side, wincing.

"All right," the nurse says. "That's it. Out, out, all of you out. She just woke up, she needs a minute, you can come back later, *one at a time* —"

Slowly, over the next few hours — or maybe it's days? — I get more information. I've got three broken ribs and two bruised ones, two fractured fingers on my right hand and six stitches in my forehead. There's no sign of major internal injury, but they want to keep an eye on me for another couple of days to make sure nothing develops, and to make sure my ribs are healing. ("These are some severe breaks, Bonnie.") I've been unconscious for two whole days. I missed graduation. Not to mention Zach's wrist surgery. Kate's stitches and concussion watch. The half a day where the doctors thought they were going to have to perform surgery to repair the bleeding around Liam's liver. In the end, they decided it wasn't needed, but they're keeping him here a few more days for observation, just in case.

"And Jack?" My hands are knotted in the thin hospital blankets as I look at Kate, who's sitting right next to me. We're the only people here. Liam went back to his room to rest and Zach went with him, because I guess they got all buddy-buddy while I was unconscious.

"Where is he?" I think of him bleeding on the ring floor. "Is he … did I …"

"No," Kate says quickly. "They took him to another

hospital. I don't know which one, and I don't know exactly how he is, but he's alive. And he doesn't know where we are."

Relief, powerful enough to make my head spin a little.

Then, "Wait. How do you know that?"

"The cops told me."

I start to sit up, then immediately regret it. "You talked to the cops?"

"They've been swarming this place since we got here. Everyone talked to them." Kate pulls at a fraying thread on the edge of my hospital blanket. "They're coming back tomorrow. To talk to you. The social worker, too."

The nurse returns to check the tape on my ribs and give me more IV fluids. Kate goes, promising to come right back after she and Zach get something to eat downstairs. Her absence leaves a weight that presses on my chest the way the calculations for the Plan used to, lying awake in Jack's apartment.

It's over.

The police must know about my involvement in the ring. Must know about Jack. Even if I'm not arrested for illegal fighting — or for beating up Jack — we'll at least be taken away from him. I won't go back into foster care with Kate and Zach. I'll be eighteen on Friday, only four days away. I could, technically, apply for guardianship. But I don't have any money or a job or somewhere to live. And of course if the police decide to charge me, that won't be an option anyway.

Liam returns. One look at me, and he's hugging me, his arms held carefully so my ribs don't twinge and our IVs don't get tangled. He leaves mysteriously and returns with peanut M&M's, which he slips me when the nurses aren't looking. Holds my hand, thumb always on my wrist, *tap, tap.*

The nurse reappears, sees the M&M's wrapper on my bed

and shoos Liam out before I have to say anything.

In the evening, Kate helps me wash my greasy hospital hair, then spends forever carefully brushing out the tangles, French braiding it. Zach reads aloud from a beat-up copy of *Percy Jackson* the nurse gave him from the lost and found. The sky turns orange and red as the sun sets. All day, the doctors and nurses have been complaining about the heat wave, which still hasn't broken.

Cots appear. Kate and Zach were discharged this morning, but since social services isn't coming until tomorrow, they're staying here with me tonight. Kate moves the two cots so they're right next to my bed, one on either side.

Tell them.

"Listen," I say, once they're both settled in. I was so nervous before the last fight, I thought I would pass out. But that's nothing compared to how I feel now. "I have to tell you guys something, okay? Tomorrow, when the cops come, I think … I think they're going to … that we'll …"

My voice cracks. Kate reaches over the guardrail on my bed and takes my IV-free hand.

"Zach and I talked already," she says. "Right, buddy?"

"Right," Zach says.

"He was worried all this was his fault. Because he called the police that night."

"What?" I turn to him. "Zach, you *saved* us. If you hadn't called when you did …"

Earlier, Kate told me he got my phone from Jack's room while Jack was destroying Kate's laptop and phone. Snuck away and grabbed it before Jack even noticed.

My brave, brave little brother.

"I told him that, too. He understands now." Kate looks at

me, eyes green and big and shining. "And we know what's coming. We're ready."

"This wasn't supposed to happen." I can barely get the words out. "I was supposed to protect you."

"Bo. You *did*. But it was too much." Kate crushes my hand. I crush hers right back. "It doesn't have to be you against the world anymore. It shouldn't have been like that in the first place."

I turn to my brother, reaching for him with my free hand. "I promised you, Zach. I promised you we'd stay together ..."

Zach fidgets with the guardrail on my bed. When he can't figure out how to lower it, he climbs over it instead, snuggling as close to me as he can get. He hiccups once. Twice.

But he says, "I'll be okay. I just don't want you to be hurt anymore."

Something fundamental in me comes undone. I shut my eyes, burying my fists in the blankets.

Zach falls asleep first. Then Kate, her cot pulled up right next to mine, my guardrail lowered so it's like one big bed. Kate snores. Zach curls against my side, fingers nestled in my hospital gown. I'm cramped and hot and my ribs hurt.

I hold them as close to me as I can.

The police arrive by 8:15 a.m. The social worker, too.

Her name is Ashley. She's wearing jeans and a pink T-shirt, and before she comes in my room, I hear her telling someone that she should've brought a sweater. She didn't realize the heat wave was going to break today, and it's cold this morning.

I hate her because I have to, but she seems okay. She offers to take Kate and Zach to McDonald's for breakfast, and when Kate looks her dead in the eye and says, "Only if I can get three McGriddles," Ashley replies, "Don't worry. That's my go-to order, too."

Neither Kate nor Zach so much as crack a smile, but I respect the effort. I guess.

Zach whispers, "I'll bring you a hash brown." And then they're gone. I tell myself it's better this way. But without them, I feel like I'm going into the ring without my gear.

There's a woman and a man. Detective Gomez and Detective Ryan. They both have neat, dark hair and wear neat, dark clothes and look exactly the way I would expect detectives to look. Detective Ryan stands by the window, fidgeting with his phone. Detective Gomez sits on the chair by my bed. She smiles at me.

"Hi, Bo. You go by Bo, right?"

I nod. Beneath my blankets, my hands are in fists. I plan on speaking as little as possible.

"You can call me Amy, if you want. That's Michael."

Detective Ryan nods. (Like I'm going to call either of them by their first names. Please.)

"You're not being charged. I want to make that very clear." Detective Gomez crosses her legs. "You don't have to talk to us if you don't want to, and you can ask for a lawyer or a social worker at any time. We can bring Ashley back. We're just trying to understand what happened. Okay?"

Again I nod. I should be relieved — they're not arresting me — but my heartbeat is tripping over itself too much to feel it.

"Let me tell you what we already know." Detective Gomez holds up her thumb. "Tyler Covey was operating an illegal fighting ring from one of the warehouses on the base. We found out about this ring after arresting a man named Derek Lee a few months ago for driving under the influence and drug possession. Our investigation into those drugs led us, eventually, to the ring. Tyler was arrested on Friday night, along with many of his associates, during a raid we launched on the warehouse."

She holds up her index finger, too. "You and Tyler's son, Liam Covey, were involved in that fight club. We have numerous eyewitnesses confirming that you fought there. Your uncle has been arrested for his involvement."

I sit up. "He has?"

"Yes. Child endangerment."

I sit back, closing my eyes, picturing Jack in handcuffs, Jack behind bars. Dizziness washes over me.

Detective Gomez clears her throat. She holds up a third finger. "You were warned, somehow, about the raid we had planned. All three of you got past us and ended up at your uncle's gym."

Fourth finger. "There were backpacks in the gym with you and the apartment upstairs was messy, suggesting some sort of attempt to run." Pinky. "After that, for reasons we don't know, you and Jack had an altercation that resulted in both of you being severely injured, as well as Liam and your siblings. Your uncle's going to make a full recovery, by the way. I don't know if anyone's told you that yet."

I flush. Jack, bleeding and motionless on the ground, because of me.

What if I'd killed him?

"At some point in the altercation," Detective Gomez continues, "your brother called 911, which is when the paramedics and police found all of you and brought you here. Obviously, there are a few gaps in our knowledge. We just want to know what happened, and why. Okay?"

When I don't say anything, Detective Gomez continues, "All right. How about we talk about your injuries, then?"

"My injuries?"

She nods. "When you were admitted, the doctors ran a lot of tests, including an MRI. They found significant evidence of past injuries. Things that your primary care doctor has no record of."

"I'm a fighter." The answer comes instinctively. "I get injured a lot."

Detective Ryan jumps in, shaking his head. "I asked Tyler about you specifically. He isn't saying much, but he had a lot to say about you."

"Me?"

He nods. "It's one thing for a bunch of adult men to get roped into this. It's completely another thing for a minor to be involved, and a girl at that. Not that girls can't also fight, but we have to be sure there wasn't also anything ... *else* going on."

My cheeks burn.

Detective Ryan clears his throat. "Tyler was very clear in his statement. You were a fighter in the ring, nothing more. You were competing in the annual tournament he hosted, which ran once a month, but you left before the final on Friday night. Which would mean that the last time you fought was — correct me if I'm wrong — April?"

I say nothing. I'm feeling slightly sick.

"You have a lot of new injuries now, it's true," Detective Gomez adds. "But some of the injuries the doctors found are older than that, or not consistent with boxing injuries.

Bruising on your ribs that looks to be at least a week old. Old bruises on your back, when boxers do not typically hit each other from behind. Bruising on your tailbone. A cut on your side that's barely healed. Not to mention these texts."

In spite of myself, I sit up as Detective Gomez holds up her phone to me. A screenshot. All of Liam's texts sent the day after Jack attacked me and took my money.

I could kick myself. Why didn't I think about what might happen if someone else read them? *Stupid.*

I push the phone away and draw my knees up.

"We're just trying to understand what happened," Detective Gomez says again. "Your uncle … I get the sense we've only scratched the surface with him. If that's true, then we want to gather all possible evidence we can so we can do the right thing. The fights are one thing. But they don't explain what happened at the gym that night. And … he's hurt, Bo. Badly. We can't ignore that. From a legal standpoint, all of this becomes a very different story — with a very different outcome for you — if you had a reason to act the way you did, or if you thought you and your siblings were in danger."

I don't realize I'm shaking until Detective Gomez puts her hand on my arm.

"You're safe, Bo," she says quietly. "He can't hurt you anymore."

I look around at where I am. My *hospital room.* I stayed all this time, faced Jack because I thought it was the only way. Because I was sure it was worth it.

Worth what? Worth Kate's bandages and Zach's cast and Liam's injuries? Worth Zach's crushingly tight hugs before every single fight, *Do you have to go back there?* and *I heard Jack yelling*, nightmares, worry never leaving his eyes? Worth Kate asking me to rate Jack's mood on a scale from one to ten, and her preparing me for every fight and cleaning me up after, and joking around with Jack, pretending it was normal, because what else could she do? Worth Liam whispering that it's too much, always looking like he could fall apart at any moment, *I worry about you all the time*? Worth what I did to Jack, him lying motionless on the floor, bleeding—

I pull my blankets down and look at my hands.

It's like I'm seeing them for the first time. Bruises, blue and black and purple and yellow. Scars — two years' worth — white and pink and everything in between. The splint on my fingers. The IV pinching the back of my hand.

Suddenly, Liam's words that morning in the truck come back to me.

I don't get why everything else matters more than what he does to you.

"Jack ..."

My voice comes out hoarse. Like even now, my body is rejecting me saying it.

But I clear my throat. Wipe my cheeks. Take a deep breath.

"He hits me."

NINETEEN

By the time I'm discharged from the hospital, I'm eighteen, and Kate and Zach have been in their foster homes for nearly a week.

Kate's in La Salida. Zach's in Berkeley. Both their foster families are nice. And they try. Hard. They set up visits and phone calls with me for as soon as tomorrow. Pretend not to stare at my bruised face and broken hand. They take me on a little tour of their homes, showing me the kitchen stocked with Kate's favorite salt and vinegar chips, the bonus room where she and her friends can hang out on weekends, the living room with a whole bookshelf of new books for Zach, the extra-clean guest bedroom made up special with new blankets and fresh paint and framed pictures of me, Kate, and Zach together. Kate is the only kid at her home, but Zach's foster parents have two baby girls — twins that Zach's always bringing toys to or making silly faces at so they smile and giggle.

I hold it together. When Kate says, "Isn't this room cute?" I hum in agreement instead of saying, *Your room in Greenville would've been bigger*. I push down my jealousy at the literal babies who will get to spend more time with my brother than I can. And I only cry a little, even when Zach hugs me as tightly as he would before a match and whispers, hiccuping, "It's not forever. Right?"

After, I take the bus to Liam's. I accepted his mom's offer to stay there until I figure out something more permanent. Liam gave me the spare key yesterday. Their house is blue with white trim, a messy yard. It's small. Only two bedrooms. I'll be crashing on the couch. Foster care would never have let Kate and Zach stay here, too.

I've barely closed the front door before it hits me: the breathlessness, the dizziness, the sweating. I slide to the floor, head between my knees and hand over my chest, feeling my heart skitter, *thu-thump thu-thump thu-thump*.

Liam wakes up from a nap and finds me there on the floor. He says a lot of things I don't hear until he says, "You're having a panic attack," and then he's on the floor next to me, breathing slowly, deeply, asking me to do the same.

"I don't know," I manage, "how to do this without them."

Telling Detectives Gomez and Ryan the truth starts a process I can't stop. There are meetings at the police station. Lots of them. Meetings with our court-assigned lawyer, Jane Wentworth. All of us — me, Kate, Zach, Liam — give statements to the police. One afternoon I sign so much paperwork that my hand cramps. Jack, who is already being charged with assault and child endangerment, gets even more charges added: child abuse, child neglect, aggravated assault, aggravated battery. There's a big article in *La Salida Times* (and even the much bigger *San Francisco Chronicle*) about the raid on the fight club, and then a follow-up about a man who coerced his niece into fighting there.

Ashley the social worker is around all the time. CPS agents, too. The police notified them about Jack, and while the cops scrutinize everything related to the ring, CPS agents handle the investigation into Jack's abuse. They ask me about a million questions, but most of them boil down to the same thing: *Why didn't you come forward sooner?*

I ask about guardianship. The CPS agent is evasive, but the next morning, after Liam and his mom both leave for work, Ashley calls me.

"I'm not sure," she says carefully, "that guardianship is a good idea for you right now."

My grip on the phone is painful. "Why not?"

She sighs. "CPS is concerned about the effect living with Jack has had on Kate and Zach, even though they weren't the ones enduring the majority of his abuse. They feel that you staying with him, not reporting him, shows you weren't mature enough to understand the consequences of that decision for Kate and Zach, and therefore you aren't ready to take care of them. And they're concerned about your own well-being. Having two kids is a lot of responsibility for anybody. Let alone someone who's been through the trauma you have."

It takes everything I have not to hurl my phone at the wall.

Of course I finally tell the truth, and it gets thrown back in my face. We *still* can't be together.

But then I remember Jack. What I did to him. I tip sideways on the couch, curling in on myself. Maybe CPS is right. I shouldn't be responsible for anyone if I can lose control like that. Hurt someone like that.

"Bo. Listen to me," Ashley says. "I know this isn't what you wanted. I know it's hard. But you can still make this happen, and I want to help. I've got a proposal for you. Do you trust me?"

I laugh.

Ashley waits. I stare at my phone. The background is a picture of Kate and Zach at our most recent visit: Zach reading a book, his head on Kate's stomach, Kate making a peace sign and a goofy face at the camera.

I remember my old promise.

Whatever it takes.

I close my eyes. "What's the plan?"

I rejoin foster care.

Ashley helps me with the paperwork. I knew, vaguely, from Jack's early guardianship days and the monthly social worker visits, that this was a thing, that you could stay in care until you were twenty-one if you wanted. But I never once considered *doing* it, so I never bothered learning the details. But Ashley promises me this will show a responsibility and maturity CPS will like. That if I do what I'm supposed to while I'm back in care — complete the programs they ask me to, work, get my own place — it will not only help my case for guardianship, but also put me in a better position to take care of my siblings than if I tried to do it all on my own.

And the rules are different, so I don't even have to live with foster parents. In fact, one of the first things they want me to do is save up enough to move into my own place, which they'll help me find.

Also, there's money. Not a lot, but some. The shoebox,

my savings, was confiscated as evidence, so I'm not getting it back. I need every penny I can get.

I enroll in a personal finance class through social services. Get two part-time jobs — one at Safeway, one at the library, doing things like shelving books and dealing with inventory. The pay's okay, but not great.

"What about boxing?" Kate asks me one evening. She calls me every night. "Couldn't you do something with that?"

My hands twitch. I still wake up at 5:00 a.m. every day, ready to train. Sometimes, when I can't sleep, I end up on my feet, shadowboxing in the dark before I realize what I'm doing and make myself stop.

But I think of bloodied, unconscious Jack.

I tell Kate, "No boxing."

When I have enough saved, I buy the cheapest car I can find. It's tiny and dented and there's no AC, but it runs just fine when I move into an apartment just on the other side of the bridge. It's a studio. Like my car, it's also tiny and dented and there's no AC.

After I close the front door, I feel the walls closing in just a little. Feel that itch in my fingers that used to send me downstairs to the gym or into the ring. I pace the empty apartment until I finally fall asleep, where I dream of the ring, of Kate's black eye and Zach's broken wrist, of Jack chasing me through the gym until I wake up gasping for air and reaching for Kate and Zach before I remember that neither of them are here.

***

On Liam's first day of college, I meet him for lunch on campus. We eat on a grassy lawn surrounded by eucalyptus trees and red-tiled roofs, the bell tower ringing. He waves his arms as he tells me all about his first two classes, biology and anatomy. Everything makes him laugh.

"I love it already. Geez. Is that crazy? Have you ever just, like, *loved* something right away like that? Hey, are you gonna eat the rest of those M&M's?"

When he kisses me goodbye, he holds my face in his hands. His fingertips are cool and soft, and I try not to think about them wiping CutPro on my skin or holding the enswell to my head. Try not to think about boxing at all.

On Zach's first day of fifth grade, I arrange things with his foster parents so I can pick him up from school. Go to the library like we used to. We keep it a surprise from Zach. I get there early so I can be right there on the sidewalk when he comes out.

But the bell rings, and Zach doesn't appear.

Five minutes pass. Ten. Fifteen.

At twenty, almost everyone else is gone. I'm about to go into the school when Zach finally emerges. A smile breaks out over his face.

"Bo!"

I crush him to me. "Where *were* you?"

"Talking to some friends." He pulls back, frowning. "What's wrong?"

Friends.

My face is warm. I busy myself with my car keys. "Nothing.

I'm just excited to see you! What were you talking with your friends about?"

Outside the library, a couple of women are handing out flyers. I try to sidestep them, but one of them catches me and presses a lilac paper into my hand.

TIME'S UP GYM: A Brand-New Women's Gym!

They boast treadmills, a full complement of weight machines, Zumba classes, and —

"You teach boxing?" The question's out of my mouth before I can stop it.

The woman beams at me. "Yes. Do you box?"

"I used to."

"Well, if you want to teach, *please* send me an application! I thought I had a teacher lined up, but she just bailed and I'm desperate for a replacement. We're looking for someone to teach a self-defense class, too. Here. Call me if you're interested."

Before I can say no, she presses a business card into my hand.

I don't dare apply for a job there. I don't want to give CPS or the family courts any reason to remember what I did to Jack, any reason to be more "concerned about my well-being."

But a week later, when I wake up from another nightmare, instead of staring at the ceiling until it's time for work, I find myself getting up. Getting dressed. Driving to Time's Up. Half a dozen women are here lifting weights or using exercise machines. The ring at the back is empty, the punching bags still.

Stretches. Jump roping. A short run on the treadmill before I put on my gloves.

Whump, whump, whump. Chain rattling. My breath in bursts. Knuckles aching, the good kind of ache, warmth in my body—

I step back, gasping for air. Automatically, I glance to each side, looking for Jack.

But there's no one. Only the other women on the machines and my own reflection in the mirror.

And I'm … okay. My hands aren't twitching. A calmness settles over me in a way I haven't felt since I left the hospital.

I lift my fists and turn back to the bag.

Jack goes to trial in October. I spend most of it trying not to look at him. Dreading my turn at the witness stand. Flinching when anyone gets too close to me, constantly reminding myself to breathe.

The whole thing is a blur until the very end, when the jury forewoman stands up and says, "Guilty on all charges," and I see the handcuffs go on Jack's wrists.

Behind me, there's crying. Liam's mom. Ashley, too, and Kate's and Zach's foster parents. Jane Wentworth reaches out to give me a hug, but Kate's and Zach's arms are already around me, squeezing me tight, my face buried in Kate's shoulder, my hands in Zach's hair.

When they let me go, Liam, who skipped class today to be here, kisses me, leaning over the rail that separates the public benches from our table to do it. Zach makes a gagging sound.

Liam pulls away. His thumb traces the scar on my forehead, just as softly as he did when he was my cutman.

"How does it feel?" he asks.

"I ... don't know."

I glance behind me, watching Jack go through the door at the back of the courtroom. He's pale, and he looks skinnier and smaller than I remember.

Jack looks back, his gray eyes locking on mine. For a moment, I can feel his hand on my shoulder, his voice in my ear.

With effort, I turn my back to him, and when I do, I'm facing my siblings. Smiling Kate, already texting her friends the news. Zach, near as always, but talking to Jane, laughing so loud he hiccups. Behind them, the courtroom doors are open, revealing a hallway window that overlooks the bay, sparkling blue in the fall sun, stretching out endlessly into the horizon.

Zach sees me looking. He takes my hand. "Are you okay?"

I smile at him. I reach for Kate, looping my arm through hers. Together, we head for the doors.

"I'm great."

ACKNOWLEDGMENTS

Writing a book — especially a debut book — is a very humbling and surreal experience. Writing the acknowledgments for that book is perhaps even more so. I'm grateful to have had the help of so many amazing people during this journey, and to be able to express that gratitude here.

For my agent, Joan Paquette: thank you for coming to Lesley, hearing the first page of this story, and inviting me to send you more when the book was done. I still pinch myself when I think about that moment. Thank you for all your time and effort pitching this story to every publisher under the sun. And thank you for being willing to call me from airports and the other side of the world to give me good news.

A huge thank-you to my editor extraordinaire Shelley Tanaka. I feel beyond lucky to have worked on my debut novel with you. Thank you for getting this book, asking the best questions, and always telling me to trim. This story became so much more than I could have ever dreamed of because of your guidance and vision.

Thank you also to Emma Sakamoto and everyone at Groundwood for all your work to bring this book to the shelves. Special shoutout to Greg Tabor for the coolest cover ever.

This book as it is now literally wouldn't exist without the insights and advice of my mentors at Lesley University. Tracey Baptiste, thank you for telling me at my very first workshop that this wasn't a fantasy story. You were right. (You're always right!) Jason Reynolds, thank you for telling me to relax. That advice changed how I write. Also, shout-out for asking me if I'd ever been punched in the face. Best workshop moment ever. Chris Lynch, thank you for having the patience to work on this story with me for a full year, for fixing the "logic holes" my stories always seem to contain, and for telling me to lean into the feminism. Also, thank you for the title!

A special thank-you to two years' worth of wonderful workshop members: Stephanie Willing, Tracy Thorpe, Jørn Otte, Andrea Voglesonger, Saraceia Fennell, Kathy Karch, Patrick Brown, Elise Hanna, Benjamin Simani, and Ellen Houlihan. (I still have all of your notes!)

And of course, the biggest thank-you to the YA All-Star Squad: Cassie Stossel, Emily Lee, and Merlyn Mayhew. Thank you for countless pep talks, notes, and brainstorming sessions over many years. Thank you for always believing in Bo, Kate, Zach, and Liam — and in me. I'm glad your Jacks are better people than mine. Let's get #Resley going soon, okay?

To my intrepid team of experts: Ruth Campbell and Sarah Swensen for their insights into social work and the foster care system; Jonathan Galindo for his boxing expertise (and for telling me to "just give her the MMA gloves"); Gary Soots and Wayland Gee for their knowledge of police and investigative protocols; and Elizabeth Huff and Beth Passey for their medical knowledge. Thank you for spending some of your time guiding me and answering my many questions. This book would be much worse off without your insights.

I may not have attempted writing a book at all if it weren't for many teachers, from kindergarten and beyond, who encouraged me to keep reading and keep writing: Claire, Michelle, Laurie, Kristin, Joanna, Jess, Julie, Stephen Tuttle, and John Bennion. A special thank-you to Julie for telling me that my short story about a girl who gets into fights at school felt like it could be part of something larger.

Also, thank you to One Direction for existing — not only are you one of my favorite bands, but a fan fiction I wrote in high school about Liam Payne eventually evolved into this boxing novel. I'm still not entirely sure how that happened, but I'm grateful that it did. Rest in peace, Liam.

Thank you to the friends who help me see myself and the world more clearly: Alexa, Garron, Reese, and Riley. I would be a much less happy person without your support, patience, excitement, and kindness — not to mention the day trips, blind karaoke nights, gifts, texts, pool parties, concerts, surprise FaceTime sessions, and endless laughter.

Alison, you get your own paragraph. Thank you for years of feedback and brainstorming sessions and for your endless patience with my many panicked texts and rambling voice memos. Thank you for always believing in the "fight club story" and in me. Bo, Liam, Kate, and Zach would be much poorer off without your passion, enthusiasm, and brilliance — as would I.

Bo would be lost without her family, and I would, too. Thank you to Mom, Dad, and Caroline for being the most patient and the most supportive family I could have asked for … even when I wouldn't let you read the book. I hope it was worth the wait, and I hope you know I could not have written this novel or come this far without the three of you. A special thank-you also to Millie, Spencer, Sid, and Frankie.

A big, big thank-you to my big, crazy, loud, and wonderful extended family, including those who have come before us.

And finally, thank you to Grammie. Thank you for all you did for yourself and your family. Thank you for always speaking up for what was right and for women and for teaching us to do the same. Thank you for your laughter, singing, cooking, shopping trips, strong opinions, and love. And thank you for believing in this story, which I could not have written without your example and influence. I hope you are proud of what it's become, and of me. Love you more.

ABBIE HARLOW has a BA from Brigham Young University and an MFA in Creative Writing from Lesley University, where *The Butterfly's Sting* was her thesis project. When she's not writing, she works in the main office of a high school, where she observes the trials and triumphs of students every day. Abbie lives in Alameda, California, inspiration for the setting of this story and where her family has lived for five generations. *The Butterfly's Sting* is her first novel.